Grandmother's Stories

from the Library of:

Verónica Córdova de la Rosa.

REDA
AL-DABBAGH

Grandmother's
Stories

TALES FROM
OLD SYRIA

WHITE MOUNTAIN

White Mountain Books is an affiliate of
The Arcadian Group S.A., Case Postale 431, 1211 Geneva 12, Switzerland
Copyright © White Mountain Books 2017

Database right White Mountain Books (maker)

First published 2017

ISBN 9781941634783

Designed and typeset by Megan Sheer

Printed in Great Britain by CPI UK,
141-143 Shoreditch High Street, London, E1 6JE

Typeset in Monotype Arcadian Bembo

I dedicate this book to the memory of
the nineteen wise and wonderful grandmothers
winding through our family line back to the tenth century.

Foreword

Many of my most vivid and cherished childhood memories are of my grandmother's stories. When I was a young child, my siblings and I would huddle around her in a circle every night to hear them. In the warmer months, we met under the star-speckled sky of the open courtyard at the heart of our home, while the fountain burbled in the background. When it was cold, we sat on the Persian carpets and cushions in the house, nudging each other as we competed to get closest to the fire.

In everyday life, my grandmother was a calm, softly-spoken woman, with kind eyes and a gentle manner. But when she told these tales, she would transform: through her voice and gestures and words, she could become a proud sultan, or a lovelorn princess, or even a wicked genie. As a storyteller, she could cause our hearts to race in delight or terror or anticipation; she could transport us to long ago and far away—to the very furthest reaches of our imaginations. Yet at the end of each evening, after the last story was told, she would always bring us back by gathering us into an embrace and bidding us goodnight.

When I was around thirteen years old, I stopped listening to my grandmother's stories. By then, I had big ambitions for myself, and I started to read newspapers and non-fiction books instead. It was a wrench not to join my younger siblings in the courtyard or by the fire, but I thought I had no need for those stories anymore: they felt childish, and I felt too grown-up for them.

I am much older than thirteen now, yet I have returned to my grandmother's stories. I am still trying to work out exactly why. Perhaps, after a long and gruelling career, I crave something more joyful and innocent. Or maybe I am tired of hearing the true and terrible stories coming from my homeland via the news. Possibly I want to show there is more to the Eastern fairy tale canon than *The One Thousand and One Nights, Aladdin* and *Ali Baba*. Or it could be that I simply want to portray the East as I remember it from my childhood; as a land rich with culture and mystery and magic. My homeland may well be irretrievably lost, bombed and burned out of existence, but I can at least take solace in memories of what it once was – a vibrant and cosmopolitan country where everyone was welcome, where neighbours and friends would gather and feast and tell stories for hours on end; the cradle of civilisation; the place from which all stories spring.

This book is not a scholarly endeavour. I do not know the origin of many of the stories contained within its pages. In the writing of this collection, I was sometimes struck by an echo of a historical event, or of another well-known fairy tale, and though I know my grandmother was influenced by the past and by narratives from beyond the borders of Syria, I also suspect a few of these stories came straight from her imagination. But I think that is the beauty of these kind of tales: they belong to every time, every place and every person; this book is simply my grandmother's interpretation—as well as my own.

It has given me enormous pleasure to recall, write and translate these stories. I have discussed the project at length with my siblings, and we have smiled, laughed and even shed a few tears while reminiscing about those evenings with our grandmother. My brothers and sisters have also helped to jog my memory: 'Do you remember the story she told about the Goat Girl?' they have said, or, 'Don't forget the tale about the Happy Shirt.' In turn, I have tested out these versions of my grandmother's stories on my own children and grandchildren, so my first readers have been young, candid and open-minded—just as my grandmother would have wanted.

I have also found it a moving experience, the creation of this book. Of course, my beloved grandmother is no longer living, but I have felt privileged to share her words with my family, and with the publication of this volume I now hope other readers will enjoy them too. I believe I was wrong to dismiss these stories as childish, when I myself was still a child. Now, I have come to see them as timeless, universal, and important—and if nothing else, they contain a little of the remarkable spirit of grandmother, as well as all the storytellers who went before her. I know now that fairy tales and fables, no matter the simplicity of their language, serve an important purpose – they connect us with our culture and our collective past. Now that so many thousands of Syrians have been made refugees, forced out to all four corners of the globe, facing destitution, despair and discrimination, I hope these tales may offer a small glimmer of consolation in reminding us all of what our life was once like.

Last but not least, I would like to offer thanks to Amanda Block, Joe Murray and Joe Quince, and indeed the rest of the team at White Mountain Books for their invaluable assistance in bringing this book to completion. My final thanks I extend to all those who read it, may you enjoy.

Contents

The Pomegranate Prince

There once lived a sultan who wished his daughter to find a husband. The princess was very beautiful, but because she was the sultan's only child, he had spoiled her, so she had grown up to be selfish and unkind.

Nevertheless, when word went out that the princess was in want of a husband, princes travelled from far and wide, over deserts and mountains and seas, to try and win her hand. The sultan, who loved his daughter very much, wanted her to marry a man she loved, and so he invited all the princes to a great feast at the palace.

The servants prepared the most magnificent meal for all the guests, which included many plates of pomegranate, a speciality of the kingdom. One of the princes, who had travelled a long way to see the princess, had never seen pomegranate before. When he first tasted the sweet red seeds, he did not think he had ever eaten anything so delicious in his life. He ate all the pomegranate on his plate and, when one seed fell onto the palace's pristine marble floor, he bent down to eat that too.

The princess, having seen what the prince had done, pointed to him and gave a shriek of laughter. Then she turned to her father, and said:

This man, he cannot be a prince,
He acts as though he's poor.

A beggar's come into my house,
To eat food off the floor!

Everyone at the feast joined in with the princess' laughter, and the pomegranate prince fled from the room, humiliated. He prepared to return home, but he could not rid his mind of the princess' beautiful face, nor her cruel words. Despite himself, he had fallen in love with her, but he also wished to teach her a lesson.

It so happened that this prince was a beautiful singer, and that his voice was so resonant that it was known to stop people in their tracks, bringing smiles to their faces and tears to their eyes. So one night, when all in the palace were sleeping, the prince crept into the garden below the princess' window and began to sing.

Roused from her sleep by the enchanting melodies, the princess went out onto her balcony and looked down upon the faraway figure singing in her garden.

'You have a beautiful voice,' she said to him. 'You may stand in the middle of the garden to sing to me.'

So the prince stood amongst the flowers and sang until his voice was hoarse, and the princess had drifted off to sleep once more.

The next night, the prince returned to the garden when all in the palace were sleeping, and began to sing once more. This time, the princess was lying awake, thinking of the mysterious man who had serenaded her the night before, so when she heard him she hurried to the balcony.

'You have a beautiful voice,' she said to him again. 'You may stand on this balcony to sing to me.'

So the prince climbed up to the window and sang in the shadows until his voice was hoarse, and the princess had drifted off to sleep.

On the third night, the princess was waiting for the mysterious man, and no sooner had he opened his mouth than she ran to greet him.

'You have a beautiful voice,' she said to him again. 'You may come into my bedroom to sing to me.'

So the prince snuck into the princess' bedroom and sang until his voice was hoarse, but the princess did not sleep. Even in the light, she did not recognise him as the pomegranate prince from the feast, for she had seen so many suitors that day. Instead, she had completely fallen in love with this stranger and his beautiful singing.

'Who are you?' she asked him. 'I must better know the man who sings to me so sweetly. What is your name?'

The prince considered this for a moment, and then decided on the most foolish name he could think of. 'Brombu,' he said. 'My name is Brombu.'

'Oh Brombu, I love you!' said the princess. 'We must be married!'

'Alas,' said the prince, 'I cannot marry you, Princess. For I am so very poor – like a beggar – and the only way I survive is by singing for coins.'

'I do not care that you are poor,' declared the princess, 'although my father will never allow me to marry a beggar. We must run away and marry, we must elope!'

So the princess and the prince, still pretending to be the beggar Brombu, ran away and were married in secret. Then, instead of taking her back to his magnificent palace in his kingdom far away, he led her to a little run-down old shack at the very edge of the city.

'This is where you live?' asked the princess, looking at the shack in horror.

'Oh yes,' said the prince. 'I cannot afford a nicer house.'

And because the princess loved the beggar Brombu, she followed the prince into the shack.

Inside, it was very dark and damp, and there was a strange smell coming from the kitchen. When the princess looked more closely, she saw that there were small piles of mouldy fruit, rotting vegetables and a little sack of grain that looked as though it were several years old.

'This is what you eat?' asked the princess, looking at the food in horror.

'Oh yes,' said the prince. 'I cannot afford better food.'

And because the princess loved the beggar Brombu, she agreed that she would eat it too.

'The trouble is,' the prince said, as they prepared for their dinner, 'I am so poor that I cannot afford any plates. So we must eat off the floor instead.'

As he emptied the little sack of grain onto the floor, the princess looked at it in horror. But because she loved the beggar Brombu, she bent down, picked up a piece of grain from the dirty wooden floor of the shack, and ate it. Triumphantly, the prince pointed at her, shrieked with laughter, and he said:

This girl, she can't be a princess,
She acts as though she's poor.

A beggar's come into my house,
To eat food off the floor!

As she recognised her own words, the princess realised that the man she had fallen in love with and married was not a beggar called Brombu, but the pomegranate prince, whom she had humiliated at the palace. She was filled with regret for how cruel she had been and, with tears in her eyes, begged the prince to forgive her. Despite her harsh words, he loved her deeply, and could see that she was truly sorry, so he took her in his arms and kissed her. Together, they returned to the palace to tell the sultan the happy news that his daughter had finally chosen a royal husband. He was so delighted, that he arranged another feast, even bigger than the last. Only this time, the pomegranate prince requested that his favourite fruit be served with every dish.

The Hyena in the Grasslands

Many years ago, a little girl went to stay with her elderly aunt, who lived in a neighbouring town on the other side of the grasslands. Unfortunately, this child was badly behaved, and especially prone to telling lies and taking things that did not belong to her. After arriving at her aunt's house, the girl stole cake from the kitchen, a ball from the garden, and even her aunt's magnificent wooden walking stick from the living room.

'You naughty girl!' cried her aunt, as she limped through the house. 'Where have you hidden my stick?'

'I haven't touched your stick!' lied the girl. 'I have never even seen it!'

But when her aunt hobbled through to her bedroom, she discovered the cane under the girl's bed, along with the stolen cake and ball.

'You are a thief and a liar!' she cried. 'Apologise to me at once!'

Yet the little girl, who was very badly behaved indeed, stamped her foot and shouted, 'I will not apologise! You are a mean old woman and I hate you! I am going back to my mother's house right away!'

Her aunt sighed. 'Calm yourself, child. You cannot leave now, it is too late and you will lose your way in the grass.'

But the little girl was now in such a temper that she didn't listen to her aunt's warning, and before the old woman could stop her she had stormed out of the house and into the grasslands.

Before long, just as her aunt had predicted, the little girl lost her way in the long grass, which was taller than her whole body. As the sky grew gloomy, she sat down on the ground and began to cry, still cross with her aunt for shouting at her, and frightened of the oncoming darkness. Then something rustled loudly in the vegetation nearby, and the little girl gave a start as a hyena crept out of the grass. He was a huge striped beast, with long limbs and coarse, spiky fur. He circled the child, his long dark snout stretching into a grin that revealed sharp yellow teeth.

'What's a little girl like you doing all alone in the grasslands at night?' he asked in a soft voice.

Attempting to be brave, the child jumped to her feet, although she was still smaller than the ferocious beast.

'My aunt was very mean to me, so I was on my way back to my mother's house on the other side of the grasslands, but I got lost.'

The hyena licked his lips, tempted to gobble her up right there and then. But he was a callous creature, and liked to play with his food before he ate it, so he said, 'I will show you the way through the grasslands and back to your mother's house.'

The girl was surprised but grateful to hear this. 'Oh thank you, thank you!' she cried.

'I have one condition,' said the hyena. 'If, for some reason, your mother does not let you inside, I will eat you up for my dinner.'

The girl was alarmed to hear this, but she did not see any reason her mother would not let her inside, so she said, 'I agree to your condition. Now please, Mr Hyena, show me the way through the grasslands.'

So the little girl and the fearsome beast set off together, winding their way through the long grass. It soon grew very dark and the child could barely see past her hands, although every so often she caught a glimpse of the hyena's beady eyes and sharp teeth glinting in the moonlight. She could feel his large, warm body moving beside hers, she could smell the stench of his fur and his rancid breath, and with every step she took she shivered with fright as much as cold.

Eventually, as he had promised, the hyena led her to the edge of the grasslands, and the little girl saw her mother's house at last. She thanked the creature, and waited for him to melt back into the wilderness, but he sat on his haunches and reminded her of their agreement: 'If, for some reason, your mother does not let you inside, I will eat you up for my dinner.'

But the little girl, who felt bolder now she was out of the long grass, merely laughed. 'There is no way my mother will not let me in,' she said, as she knocked on the door.

Unfortunately, she had forgotten how late it was, and her mother was not expecting a visitor in the middle of the night, so she did not hear the knocking. The hyena edged closer.

'I will give you two more chances before I eat you,' he said.

As her heart drummed with fear, the girl knocked as loudly as she could on the door, in the hope it would wake up her mother inside the house. To her relief, a few moments later, a voice called out from the upstairs window.

'Who is that, knocking at my door at this late hour?'

'Mother, it is me, your daughter!' cried the little girl.

'Nonsense, my daughter is staying with her aunt, my dear older sister,' replied her mother. 'Now go away and leave me to sleep!'

The hyena edged closer still to the little girl and licked his lips once more.

'I will give you one more chance before I eat you,' he said.

The child knocked on the door for the third time.

'Mother!' she shouted. 'Mother, it is me, your daughter! Please, let me in! There is a hyena outside, and he is going to eat me!'

Again, a voice called out from the upstairs window: 'That does sound like you, my daughter, but you are telling lies, as usual – a hyena would eat a little thing like you on sight! Besides, why are you here when you are supposed to be with your aunt? You must have been naughty, as you always are, so as punishment you can sit on that doorstep until dawn.'

'No more chances,' said the hyena, and he pounced.

The girl screamed and struggled, but the fearsome creature was too strong for her, and with a sharp close of his great jaws he bit off her left foot.

'I will start at the bottom,' he said, crunching on her bones, 'and I will work my way up to your head.'

But just as he pulled the child towards him for a second bite, a shape appeared in the darkness behind him. There was a great thwacking noise, and the hyena collapsed to the ground.

'Auntie!' cried the little girl, for she saw it was her mother's sister who had appeared from the edge of the grasslands.

The old woman did not answer: she stood over the hyena and whacked him over the head with her walking stick again and again, until the creature finally rolled over and died.

Afterwards, when they had been let inside, the little girl's aunt explained she had been very worried after their quarrel, when her niece had run off into the wilderness on her own, so she had hurried through the dark grasslands to protect her, and was very sorry she had not arrived in time to save the little girl's foot. The child's mother was sorry too, and wished she had opened the door sooner, only she had thought the story about the hyena another of her daughter's lies. But nobody was sorrier than the little girl herself, who knew the loss of her foot was a direct result of her bad behaviour: her lies, her thieving, her temper and her disobedience.

'I promise I will be good from now on,' she told her mother and aunt. 'I promise I'll never be naughty again.'

As the months passed, and the little girl remained true to her word, her aunt gifted her the magnificent walking stick. The child was delighted, for it meant she could move about more easily on her right foot, but it also served as a reminder of her life-changing encounter with the hyena in the grasslands.

THE RIDER FROM THE NORTH

Long ago, there lived an unhappy princess. Her father's kingdom was found at the very north of the map, where it was especially cold, and the mountains were often covered in thick coats of snow. The princess, whose name was Ella, loved this beautiful land, and on fine days, she would take her magnificent chestnut horse riding for hours and hours, wrapped up in a furry hat and cape to protect herself from the chilly wind.

So it was not the country that was the cause of her unhappiness, but her father, the king, who was strict and unfeeling. One day, when Ella was sixteen years of age, he declared she was to be wed to a prince from a neighbouring kingdom. But Ella had met her intended husband before, and had disliked him immensely, for he was an arrogant and aggressive man, and ten years her senior. So she told her father she did not want to marry this unpleasant prince, and the king grew very angry.

'Your disobedience shames me, Ella,' he said. 'As long as you remain my daughter, and as long as you live in my kingdom, you will do as I command – and I command you to marry this prince.'

The king was confident these words would quash his daughter's rebellious spirit, but they had the opposite effect: that night, Ella crept from her bed, packed a bag of supplies, and stole into the stables, where she saddled her chestnut horse and galloped away from the only home she had ever known.

'I leave your kingdom and I cease to be your daughter,' she whispered over her shoulder, toward the palace that grew smaller and smaller behind her, 'and so, you can command me no longer, father.'

It took Ella several days to leave her father's land, and once she had crossed the border she continued to ride, unsure of where she should go and what she should do. After all, she had spent all of her sixteen years as a princess, and had never considered she might be anything else.

Ella had never been a vain or materialistic girl, so she was not too concerned when her clothes became worn and her long white-blonde hair became tangled from days and days of riding. She did not care she no longer looked like a princess, and no longer had any possessions to her name: all that mattered to Ella was that she had her beloved horse, and the whole world to explore. She did not even worry when the meagre supplies she had smuggled from the palace ran low, for strangers were kind, and offered her bread, cheese and meat for her journey, and when she was in wilder, more remote places, Ella learned to live off the land as resourcefully as any animal. She picked fruits and berries from the trees, vegetables and herbs from the soil, and even managed to spear fish from the rivers.

So all in all, Ella's journey from her home was a great adventure, and although it was tough at times, a little coldness or hunger could never detract from the experience of seeing so many new places, and sleeping under the stars. The only emotion that ever caused Ella to doubt what she was doing was loneliness. Though she was pleased to be away from her tyrannical father, she missed her friends from the palace, and as she was always moving, she never felt any real connection to the people she met along the way, no matter how generous they were. Every night, as she snuggled against her horse for warmth, she told herself she should find somewhere to settle and start a new life, but her heart told her she had not found that place yet, and so in the morning she always rode on.

Without really being aware of it, Ella had travelled in a south-easterly direction, and after many months on the road, the landscape around her began to look very different from that of her father's kingdom. Here, there were no more snow-capped mountains, and instead the land was flatter, and the weather dryer and hotter. Until eventually, Ella found herself on the edge of an expanse of desert, which was both enthralling and imposing to the northern princess.

After a few days of tentatively exploring this strange new landscape, Ella noticed a girl of her own age trudging through the sand, a large pot balanced on her head. She rode up to the stranger and waved in greeting, and the girl was so surprised by the sudden appearance of a blonde-haired, fair-skinned person atop a horse that her pot tumbled from her head and the water it contained seeped at once into the dry sand. Immediately, Ella jumped from her horse and tried to apologise, but she had ridden so far that she and the girl did not speak the same language. So instead she offered her own water, and a few dates and nuts from her pack, which the other girl gratefully accepted.

Over the next hour or so, through a mixture of sign language and simple drawings in the sand, Ella learned the girl's name was Maja, and that she hailed from a nomadic desert clan. When Ella expressed surprise that Maja had been carrying a pot so large, Maja managed to explain that the women of the clan were always sent to fetch water from any oases they encountered, while the men lazed in their tents. Ella thought this very unfair, and frowned her disapproval, but Maja merely shrugged, and the former princess took this to mean that was the way it had always been.

For her part, Maja was fascinated by Ella's beautiful chestnut horse, and implied she had never seen such an animal before. When Ella asked how the clan travelled, Maja drew a four-legged creature in the sand that might have been a horse, were it not for the two humps on its back, and explained to Ella this animal was called a camel.

Although both Ella and Maja were around the same age, they were so different that each was fascinated by the other. Ella was, therefore, very pleased when Maja indicated she should follow her to the camp and meet the rest of her clan. But first, the two girls walked back towards the oasis that Maja had recently left, and refilled her pot of water, so she would not return to her people empty-handed.

The men and women of the desert clan turned out to be just as intrigued by Ella as Maja had been, and they plucked at her white-blonde hair and reached out to touch her pale skin, which was now pink and freckled from the sun. Ella too was intrigued by their dark hair and olive skin, the long robes they wore, and their large tents, which were dressed with carpets and cushions. She also came face to face with the hairy, sandy-coloured, hump-backed beasts they called camels.

It was such a pleasant exchange of cultures that the clan chief invited Ella to stay with them a while. That night, he hosted a feast in her honour, and everyone gorged themselves on stuffed lamb, sticky figs and sweet tea. Then, over the next few days, Ella ingratiated herself with the women, helping them to fetch water and cook, trying to learn snippets of their language, and even teaching Maja and the braver girls to ride her chestnut horse, which was a far sleeker and faster creature than any camel. By the time the chief decided to move on from that spot in the desert, Ella was so popular among the women that nobody questioned her decision to move on with them, as in spite of her markedly different appearance, she was now an honorary member of the group.

So the years passed, and for the most part Ella was content. After a miserable childhood under her father's rule, and the loneliness of the days she had spent travelling, she was now part of a close-knit community. In the nomadic women and some of the men, she found a replacement family, and although she and Maja had been friends from the off, they were now closer than ever, considering Ella had quickly picked up the desert people's language.

There were just two things that caused Ella unhappiness. The first was the ridiculous tradition of sending the women to fetch water, while the chief – who was a fat and lazy individual – lounged around in his tent with the most important men of the tribe.

'It just does not seem fair that those big strong men do not help at all,' Ella told Maja, over and over again.

But Maja always merely shrugged in response. 'Let it go, Ella,' she advised her friend. 'It is the way it has always been, and they are too stubborn to change.'

The other blight on Ella's happiness was of a more serious nature. Out in the harsh and unforgiving desert, food and water was scarcer than the former princess had ever known it, and therefore there was competition among those who lived there. Her clan were generally a peaceful people, but every so often a rival tribe would ride in on camels, their sabres gleaming in the sunlight, and steal all of the supplies they could lay their hands on. The men of Ella's clan would fight back as best they could, but often there would be casualties, blood would stain the sand, and usually her friends would come out worse, for they simply did not have the numbers to fight back against these invaders.

This troubled Ella to such an extent that one night she went to speak to the chief in his tent, even though, as a woman, she was not welcome there.

'I have some observations, as an outsider,' announced Ella.

The chief frowned at her. Now the novelty of her appearance had worn off, he found he was not fond of the foreigner who had ridden in on her strange animal from a distant land, and now seemed to have a great hold over the women of his clan.

'I do not see why I should listen to your observations, seeing as you are just that – an outsider,' he said.

Ella bowed her head, defeated. But the chief's son, Rakan, who had a more patient and open-minded nature than his father, leaned forward and said, 'Why not let her speak? It might be interesting to hear the observations of an outsider.'

The chief frowned still further, but gave a grunt that Ella took as an invitation to continue. Nodding gratefully to Rakan, she said, 'I cannot help but notice that you do not always have enough men to defend yourselves from these raids.'

'I do not need an outsider to tell me that,' growled the chief. 'Tell me, foreigner, how do you propose we expand our defences when we have no more men?'

'I propose you use women,' said Ella.

A shocked silence followed this proclamation, and then the chief began to roar with laughter. Soon, all of his advisors had joined in, and the only people in the tent not laughing were Ella and the chief's son Rakan, who looked thoughtful.

'I do not see what is so funny,' said Ella, the colour rising to her pale face. 'The women of this clan are brave, and strong – they have to be, to lug all the water around for you.' She did not add that the women were also far less lazy. 'I am aware we might not have the same physical prowess as men,' Ella continued, 'but if you bought some horses, like mine, and we trained with bows and daggers instead of sabres, we could be quicker, we could be—'

'Enough!' shouted the chief, his face contorted in rage. 'What is this nonsense? Women going into battle? Horses instead of camels? Bows and daggers instead of sabres? Who do you think you are, coming into my tent and speaking to me of this madness?'

'Father—' began Rakan, but the chief held up a hand to silence him.

'Get out of my sight,' he told Ella. 'Leave my tent this instant, and if I ever hear of this again, I will expel you from this clan, and you will find out how difficult it is to survive in the desert alone.'

Biting back a retort, Ella left the chief's tent, but she was furious. If only the chief would listen, she thought angrily; if only he saw the value of half of his clan. But then, perhaps she didn't need him to listen. As a princess, she was not used to being told no, and even though she had cast off her old title and the person she had been, she was still a defiant character.

So that night, while the men were asleep and the weather was cooler, Ella gathered the women together with the help of Maja, and explained her plan.

'This clan needs more people to defend it, and you are all more than up to the task,' she told them. 'I believe if we train with bows and daggers, we can be just as ferocious as the men, and if we can get hold of some horses we might even be faster.'

The women were impressed and excited by this idea, and all who were fit and able began to train with Ella for a few hours every night. Before long, they had become stronger, faster, and although they were self-taught, most could shoot a fleeing antelope with an arrow, or else fell a fox with a swipe of her dagger.

They kept these activities secret for several months, but then one night Rakan was drawn from his tent by their whoops and cheers, and he realised Ella and the other women were directly disobeying the orders of the chief.

'Oh, please do not tell your father,' Ella begged him. 'At least, not yet.'

Rakan hesitated: he knew his first loyalty should be to his blood, and his chief, but he saw the sense in Ella's idea. Besides, for some time now, he had been in love with her, this stranger from a faraway land whose spirit seemed to shine as bright as her hair.

'I will not tell,' he said. 'But in return, answer me this: is it true what the women say about you? Are you really a princess from the north?'

'I was,' replied Ella. 'But now I am part of your clan, and my fate is entwined with yours. That is why I am working to protect us.'

Not only did Rakan keep her secret, he also helped convince his father to let the women buy some beautiful horses the next time they passed through a caravanserai at the edge of a nearby village. The chief did not know what Ella intended to do with these animals, and as she was an expert at identifying good breeds, and haggled excellent prices for them, he begrudgingly admitted it did no harm to exchange some young camels for horses.

After that, Ella used the horses to gallop into opposing clans – those who had been ransacking her own for years long before she had arrived from the north – and battled their elders. When they fell, and all of their sabres lay in the sand at the feet of the formidable women standing over them, they expected death. But Ella was merciful, and offered peace instead. Realising that they were immeasurable against the might of these female warriors, they agreed at once, and Ella's clan enjoyed a period of peace.

Then one afternoon, when the group was back in the wilds of the desert, one of the chief's men saw riders on the horizon. As they drew closer, it became apparent these strangers – who outnumbered the men of the clan two to one – were clothed in black robes, were already holding their sabres aloft, and were intending nothing but malice.

'Men, to your camels!' shouted the chief. 'Defend our supplies! Defend our clan!'

Rakan and the rest of the men hurried to obey him. They threw the tents and supplies from the camels' backs, leapt between the humps themselves, and then kicked at the beasts to rush at the enemy, scattering sand in their waste.

Ella watched them go, her heart hammering in her chest.

'Women, to your horses!' she cried. 'Defend our men! Defend our clan!'

The fight was already fierce by the time Ella had saddled her chestnut horse and galloped into the fray, the rest of the women at her heels. The golden sand was stained with blood, and a few camels from both sides had already been knocked down, their riders lying injured or worse on the ground nearby. Ella saw Rakan fighting three of the black-robed strangers at once, and although he was a skilled warrior, they were wearing him down. As she sped towards them, Ella drew her bow, and seconds later, the man whose sabre had been slashing towards the chief's son had toppled from his camel, an arrow in his chest.

This single shot signalled the arrival of the women into the fray, and they steered their horses towards the attackers, their bows and daggers raised. At first, it was merely the element of surprise that worked in their favour, for the strangers were completely dumbfounded to see armed women speeding towards them on horseback. But soon enough, the enemy also discovered the women were just as ferocious as the men, and their steeds nimbler than the camels. After sustaining heavy casualties, the leader of the black-robed army called his surviving men together, and they limped away, besieged by a storm of arrows.

Afterwards, when the dead and wounded had been tended too, and most of the clan had collapsed, exhausted, to the ground, the chief slid from his camel and pointed an accusing finger at Ella.

'You!' he cried angrily. 'You disobeyed me.'

'Father, she saved my life,' said Rakan, pulling himself to his feet. 'She saved most of our lives. Without her, we would have perished or been enslaved.'

'She disobeyed me!' spat the chief, drawing his sabre. 'For that, she must be punished!'

But Rakan stood between the weapon and Ella. 'If you banish her, if you exile her to the desert, I will go with her. She is part of our clan, and our fate is entwined with hers.'

Recognising her own words, Ella's heart was moved, and she was filled with gratitude and love for the chief's son.

'I will go with her too,' said Maja, moving to stand beside Ella.

'And I!' shouted two more of the women.

'And I!' echoed more.

'And I!'

Until almost the whole of the clan, both women and men, were standing in solidarity with the girl from the north, looking back at their chief with defiance in their eyes. The old man, seeing he was beaten, dropped his sabre and hung his head.

'I see how it is,' he said. 'I see that I am the one who must be cast out into the desert.'

But Ella stepped forward and offered him her hand. 'I do not wish that at all. I only sought to show how women can defend this clan just as well as any man, just as men will be able to fetch water just as well as any woman. If you agree to these changes, I do not see why we cannot carry on together.'

The chief allowed her a small smile. 'Very well, you have my word, Ella of the North,' he said. 'Or should I say, Ella of the Clan.'

From that day, as the chief promised, the men began to help with the collection of water, meaning the task was completed in half the time, the women were fully trained, and more horses were bought. Although, as it turned out, the clan rarely needed defending after the women's first fight, for they had gained such a fearsome reputation throughout the desert that hardly anybody dared to raid them again.

Ella, meanwhile, knew she had found her place at last, and that with these nomadic people she could settle into a community, continue to travel with a tribe she loved, and experience adventure in changing landscapes. With the blessing of the chief, she married Rakan, and became a princess once more – only this time, she was Ella, Princess of the Desert.

The Angel in the Forest

Once upon a time, deep in the forest, there lived a woodcutter, his wife, and their two daughters.

The woodcutter was a strong, hardworking man. Every day, he chopped up tree trunks and branches, and every week he piled logs onto the back of his cart and made the long journey through the forest to the nearest village to sell firewood.

The woodcutter's wife was a kind, clever woman. While her husband laboured outside with his axe, she kept their little wooden house clean and tidy, prepared delicious meals on the stove, and taught their daughters to read and write and do arithmetic, for the school in the nearest village was too far away for them to attend.

The two girls, whose names were Zeina and Najda, were sweet, joyful children. When they were not studying or helping their mother in the kitchen, they would trap animals for dinner or play together in the forest beyond their home, the trees of which were so big that ten people could have surrounded one of their trunks, and if they stretched out their arms, their fingers would not touch.

Although their home was remote, the woodcutter and his family considered themselves lucky to dwell in such beautiful surroundings, and although their lives were humble, they were happy and content. Until one day, when the woodcutter's wife became very ill. Zeina and Najda put her to bed and cared for her as their father hurried to the village for a doctor, but by the time he returned, their beloved mother was dead.

In the months that followed, it felt as though a shadow had passed over the little family in the forest. The woodcutter no longer felt strong, and could barely summon the energy to lift his axe. His daughters no longer felt joyful, and ceased playing and trapping animals among the trees. The little wooden house, which had once been warm and welcoming, became cold and fell into disorder. Without the woodcutter's wife, there were no lessons, no proper meals, and there was no laughter. Soon, the woodcutter stopped going into the village to sell his firewood, and although he was too consumed with grief to realise it, he and his daughters were close to ruin.

Then one day, an angel appeared. She was not a real angel, but she was the most beautiful woman the mourning family had ever seen, with long blonde hair and clear green eyes. She had been collecting flowers in the forest, and curiosity had drawn her towards the isolated little wooden house, although she had been shocked by what she had found inside: the rooms were messy and covered in dust; the hearth was empty of firewood, and the woodcutter and his two girls were sat in dirty clothes, their stomachs rumbling with hunger.

'Dear, dear,' said the newcomer, putting some broth onto the stove and taking up a broom. 'What a terrible state this house is in. I cannot abide mess, I must set it right.'

For the next three days, she cooked, cleaned and mended, she helped the woodcutter with his work and the girls with their studies, and in doing so the kindly stranger earned the nickname of 'Angel'. By the end of the third day, and in spite of his grief, the woodcutter had fallen in love with her, and he asked the beautiful visitor to stay on in the little house as his wife.

'I will marry you,' said Angel, 'but I have a house of my own, on the very edge of the forest. Why don't you and your daughters come and live with me there? It is nearer the village, so it will be easier for you to sell your firewood, and the girls can attend school.'

The woodcutter agreed to this at once, but Zeina and Najda, who were still mourning their mother, were unsure.

'It is a lovely house,' said Angel. 'There are silk carpets on the floors, the beds have mattresses made of the softest eiderdown, and there is a whole room full of toys. Best of all, there is a grate in the garden, over which I like to barbecue all sorts of delicious food.'

Upon hearing this, the two girls, who were cold, bored and hungry, not to mention tired of living in the squalor of their once-cosy home, agreed their father could marry Angel, and they could all live together at the edge of the forest.

As soon as they arrived at Angel's house, Zeina and Najda saw she had been telling the truth, and it was just as lovely as she had promised. The silk carpets felt luxurious under their feet, the eiderdown mattresses were as soft as clouds, and the playroom was full of every toy imaginable. That evening, Angel prepared a magnificent feast on her barbecue, and the family tucked into skewers of succulent meat straight from the fire.

As the weeks went by, the girls grew fonder and fonder of Angel. They did not love her as they had loved their mother, and she was not quite as kind or clever, but she always kept the house spotless and ensured they had plenty to eat, especially from her barbecue in the garden. Moreover, while Angel was very beautiful, she was not a vain woman, and Zeina and Najda could find no mirrors in the whole of the house.

Then one night, after Angel had asked her to sweep out the ashes from beneath the grate, Najda, who was the younger of the sisters, noticed something very strange. As she pushed the broom beneath the cold grill, she caught sight of what looked like the charred remains of an ear in the cinders. Alarmed, she ran to her older sister.

'Zeina! Zeina! I found an ear in the barbecue!' she said.

Her sister laughed. 'Was it from a sheep or a cow?' she asked.

But Najda shook her head. 'It was pink and round, almost like a human ear.'

'You must have been mistaken,' said Zeina, 'it must have been a pig's ear.'

But the next night, after Angel had asked Zeina to sweep out the ashes from beneath the grate, the older girl noticed something very strange. As she pushed the broom beneath the cold grill, she caught sight of what looked like the charred remains of a toe in the cinders. Horrified, she told her sister, and together they went to their father.

'Baba! Baba! We found a toe in the barbecue!' they said.

Their father laughed. 'Was it from a cat or a bear?' he asked.

But his daughters shook their heads. 'It was long and thin, almost like a human toe.'

'You must have been mistaken,' said the woodcutter, 'it must have been a monkey's toe.'

But the girls did not believe him, and when they went back to search through the ashes under the grate, they discovered a nose, a finger with a ring still attached, and even an eyeball.

'Angel has been feeding us human flesh!' they cried to their father. 'She must be some kind of monster!'

But the woodcutter, who was very much in love with his new wife, did not believe them.

'How dare you make up these wicked stories about your stepmother, who has been nothing but good to you!' he said. 'I do not want to hear another word about it! I am leaving for a few days, to collect logs from our old house in the forest, and I expect you to behave yourselves when I am away!'

Zeina and Najda begged him not to go, but their father grew angry, and left for the forest without saying goodbye.

'What are we going to do?' Najda asked her older sister.

'We need proof,' replied Zeina. 'Then Baba will believe us.'

But when they returned to the grate in the garden, all of the ashes had been swept away, along with the nose, finger and eyeball. Undeterred, the sisters decided to creep into Angel's bedroom when their stepmother was in the village, and see what they could discover there. As with the rest of the house, the room was clean and tidy, although a sharp and unpleasant smell hung in the air.

Zeina opened a wardrobe to the right of the door, and let out a scream of alarm.

'Najda! This wardrobe is full of men's clothes, and they are covered in blood!'

Trembling, her sister opened a wardrobe on the left of the door, and gave a shriek of terror.

'Zeina! This wardrobe is full of women's clothes, and they are also covered in blood!'

Whimpering, the two sisters opened the last wardrobe together: inside there were scores of children's and even babies' clothes, all of them covered in blood.

This time, neither of the girls had a chance to cry out, for there came the sound of footsteps on the stairs: Angel had returned. In panic, the sisters looked around for a place to hide, and realised they had no choice but to bundle themselves into the nearest wardrobe, though it made them sick to their stomachs to squat among the bloody clothes.

Trying to keep as quiet as possible, Zeina and Najda watched their stepmother through a gap between the doors of the wardrobe. She walked towards her dressing table, reached into a drawer, and pulled out a handheld mirror. The girls were surprised to see this object, for there were no mirrors in the house, but when Angel raised it to her face, they realised why: the glass did not reflect the Angel they could see – a beautiful young woman with long blonde hair and clear green eyes – but a monstrous creature, with shiny black skin and red eyes that burned like embers. Their stepmother was not an angel, but an evil genie.

The girls stuffed their hands over their mouths to keep from crying out and giving themselves away, and they hardly dared breathe until the creature had left the room. Then they fell out of the wardrobe and hurried down the stairs, intending to run out of the house and towards the safety of the village. But their stepmother was waiting at the door, blocking the way out.

'There you are, girls!' she said, with a bright smile. 'I think it's time for dinner, don't you?'

The sisters' teeth chattered with fear as Angel shooed them into the kitchen. Was she about to chop them up and roast them over the barbecue, as she had all the men, women and children whose clothes now hung in the wardrobe upstairs? But, to their great relief, Angel presented both of them with a bowl of soup and a large chunk of bread.

'Eat up! Eat up!' she said. 'You are both far too skinny!'

With their spoons shaking in their hands, the girls ate a little of their soup, although they were terrified to think what ingredients it might contain. How were they going to get out of here? Then Zeina had an idea: when Angel's back was turned, the older girl took a spoonful of soup and threw it at Najda, so it dripped down her dress.

'Hey!' cried her younger sister.

But Zeina ignored her protestations, and spilled soup down her own dress as well. When Angel turned around, she took in the sight of the sisters' dirty clothes with a disgusted expression.

'You silly girls!' she cried. 'You know I cannot abide mess! Run down to the river and wash your dresses immediately.'

Upon hearing this, Zeina grabbed her sister by the hand, and they hurried out of Angel's house and towards the river. As they stripped down to their undergarments to scrub at their dresses, each girl noticed that her sister was much plumper than she had been a few weeks ago.

'Why, Angel has been fattening us up!' said Zeina. 'That is why she has been feeding us so much!'

'We have to run away,' said Najda. 'We must hurry to the village and tell them what she is.'

'But what about Baba?' replied Zeina. 'He is under her spell, and if he returns and we are not there, she might eat him instead!'

Though they had parted with him on bad terms, both girls loved their father very much, and they could not bear the thought of leaving him in danger.

'Then there is only one thing to do,' said Najda. 'We must trap her, so we can prove to Baba and everyone else that she is an evil genie.'

Once they had beaten their dresses dry, the girls set to work on the biggest trap they had ever dug, and when they had finished they covered it with twigs and leaves, so it was hardly noticeable from the rest of the forest path. Then they waited and waited, and when it was almost dark, Angel appeared, a furious expression on her beautiful features.

'Where have you girls been?' she demanded. 'You went down to the river hours ago! I thought something terrible must have happened!'

But the girls were not fooled by her pretence of kindness any longer.

'We know what you are, Angel!' cried Zeina.

'We've seen the body parts in the grate, and the bloody clothes in your wardrobe!' cried Najda.

For a moment, Angel looked shocked. Then her clear green eyes flashed red, she hissed with anger, and she started towards them. But she did not notice the loose leaves and twigs on the path between her and the sisters. When her foot fell on the twigs, she gave a shriek of alarm and the ground gave way. Zeina and Najda scurried to the pit's edge and peered down into it. There, staring up from the bottom of the trap, were the genie's burning red eyes. She screamed and screamed, attempting to climb up the muddy walls, but she could not get out.

The girls waited by the trap all night and for most of the next day, when their father, who had returned from their little house deep in the forest, found them.

'Girls!' he gasped. 'I have been looking everywhere for you! Where have you been? And where is your stepmother?'

Zeina and Najda began to explain to him what had happened, but Angel, hearing his voice, called up to him.

'My love! My life! Your daughters have played such a cruel trick on me: they have kept me in this trap all night! Help me, dearest one, I am so cold and tired and hungry!'

Upon hearing this, the woodcutter grew extremely angry with his daughters.

'How dare you do such a wicked thing to your stepmother? She has been nothing but good to you!'

'Baba, please, she's dangerous!' cried Zeina.

'Baba, please, you have to believe us!' cried Najda.

But the woodcutter ignored his two daughters' protestations, and jumped down into the trap to help his second wife. In her fight to clamber out of the pit, Angel had become entangled in the branches, and the woodcutter pulled his axe from his back to free her. When Najda saw this from above, she had an idea.

'Baba, look at her reflection in the axe!' she called down. 'Angel is not who she says she is!'

The woman quickly tried to shield her face, but it was too late. There, in the axe's blade, the woodcutter's eyes grew wide and white as he saw, not a beautiful blonde woman with clear green eyes, but a monstrous creature, with slimy dark skin, long ears, and scarlet eyes that burned like embers.

Hideously, Angel began to laugh. 'I was planning on eating your daughters first,' she said, 'for their meat will be far more tender than yours. But perhaps I will have to start with a skewer of woodcutter instead.'

To the man's horror, what he thought was his wife, a woman of melting beauty, began to transform before his very eyes into the terrible genie she truly was. Heart thumping, the woodcutter's mind raged like a stormy sea. Was this really happening? He stepped back in fear, but he could go no further. His back thudded into the muddy wall, and dark, earthy soil fell onto his shoulders – there was nowhere to go. The genie, her eyes flaring with murderous glee, her clawed hands held up toward his throat, loomed over him. As his wild eyes darted like pinballs, the woodcutter glimpsed in the reflection of his axe the faces of his two daughters, and it renewed his strength. Setting his jaw, eyes fixed, the woodcutter's fingers turned white as snow as he gripped the handle of his axe with tremendous force, and with a swing of it, Angel the genie's head was chopped clean off. Black blood spurted from the stump of her neck, an acrid smell filled the pit, and then the creature disappeared in a puff of red smoke.

Sobbing with relief, Zeina and Najda helped their father from the trap, and they fell into an embrace. The woodcutter apologised again and again for not believing them, and for marrying such a monstrous woman, especially so soon after the death of their mother. Then they went back to Angel's house, packed up their meagre belongings, and after informing the village authorities of what had happened, headed back towards their little house deep in the forest.

THE GOAT GIRL

Once upon a time, there lived a woman who had not been blessed with good looks. She had a long face, large ears and hair sprouting from her chin. As a result of her unfortunate appearance, nobody wanted to marry her, and this made the woman especially sad, because what she desired above all things was a child.

As time went on, and no suitors approached her, the woman decided to take matters into her own hands. She went to the least attractive man in the village, who ran the vegetable stall in the market, and ask him to marry her. But when he heard what she had to say, he burst out laughing.

'Marry *you*?' he jeered. 'You are aware you are no great beauty?'

'I am,' said the woman calmly, for she had developed a thick skin over the years. 'But then, neither are you very handsome.'

This was true: the vegetable seller had squint yellow eyes, large protruding teeth, and was very long-limbed and bony.

'I would like a child more than anything in the world,' the woman continued. 'If you marry me, I will help you on the stall, I will cook delicious meals with your vegetables, I will do anything you want. All I desire in return is a baby.'

The vegetable seller scratched his head. It was not a conventional or romantic proposal, but he saw there was a sense in what she was saying. Besides, he was not so deluded that he thought he would receive a better offer. So he agreed, and they were married the following day, much to the amusement of the villagers, who laughed behind their hands whenever they saw the unattractive pair.

Just as the woman had hoped, she gave birth to a baby girl not a year later. But if she had thought her and her husband's regrettable appearances might cancel one another out in the looks of their newborn, she was very much mistaken. In fact, it turned out to be quite the opposite, and it was clear from early on that their little girl was alarmingly ugly. Unfortunately, she had inherited all of her parents' worst traits – her mother's long face, big ears and hairy chin, and her father's squint yellow eyes, large protruding teeth, and bony body – and though they named her Gaitha, she was known throughout the village as the Goat Girl.

Gaitha's mother loved her very much, in spite of her appearance, but her father was not fond of his ugly daughter, just as he was not fond of his unattractive wife. As Gaitha grew up, and everybody sang 'Goat Girl! Goat Girl!' wherever she went, the vegetable seller's face burned with shame, and he cursed the day he had let his wife talk him into marrying her. Until eventually, he could no longer stand being a figure of ridicule, and so he packed up his stall and prepared to start again in a neighbouring village.

'I gave you your child,' he told his wife, before he left, 'I have fulfilled my side of our bargain.'

The woman was not sad to see him go, for she had never been fond of the unfortunate-looking vegetable seller, but she worried what would become of her daughter. She was not so blinded by affection that she was unaware Gaitha would have even less luck attracting suitors as she had. Furthermore, without a father, not to mention a father's income, the despairing mother did not think it at all likely anybody would want to marry her ugly daughter.

Gaitha, however, had other ideas. Because she had endured teasing and name-calling all her life, she had grown up to be a headstrong, spirited young woman, and when she reached the age of eighteen, she decided it was time to find a husband.

'But I will not make the same mistakes as you, mother,' she said. 'First, I will find a man who is perfect to look at, so his appearance may counterbalance my own, and second I will only marry him if I fall in love with him.'

Gaitha's mother privately thought this was a very ambitious plan indeed. But because she loved her daughter she said nothing of her reservations, and wished Gaitha luck in her romantic endeavour.

It did not take long for the news that Gaitha the Goat Girl was looking for a husband to reach the rest of the village, and people doubled up with laughter when they learned the ugly young woman was looking for someone 'perfect to look at'.

'Who is she to make such demands?' they sneered. 'She who has squint eyes and wonky teeth and a hairy chin!'

For daring to hope for an attractive husband, the villagers decided to teach Gaitha a lesson. They convinced the most handsome man among them to present himself to the Goat Girl and declare his love, so after she had fallen for him, they could all laugh at her foolishness.

The man they chose was called Zaman, and he was indeed very attractive, with smooth skin, almond-shaped eyes, and shiny dark hair. In front of a large crowd in the marketplace, he approached Gaitha and sang:

Goat Girl, oh Goat Girl,
For you I do pine!
So Goat Girl, oh Goat Girl,
Assure me you're mine!

The gathered crowd sniggered among themselves, eagerly anticipating Gaitha's glee at being courted by such a handsome man. How funny it would then be, when he turned around and rejected her! But after Gaitha had looked up at Zaman, the dazzling youth before her, she sang:

Suitor, oh Suitor,
I can't be for you,
For Suitor, oh Suitor,
Your nose is askew.

Zaman clamped a hand to his face, wailing in distress; he had always been self-conscious about his slightly crooked nose, but because he was handsome he thought nobody had noticed it. He dashed from the marketplace, his face burning with embarrassment, and Gaitha shrugged and carried on with her day.

The villagers, meanwhile, were annoyed they had been denied their fun. They could not believe someone as ugly as Gaitha could be so picky, so they decided to try again. They convinced an even handsomer man than Zaman, this one from the next village, to present himself to the Goat Girl and declare his love, so after she had fallen for him, they could all laugh at her foolishness.

This youth was called Rahil, and he was indeed very attractive, with fine features, sharp cheekbones and, most importantly, a perfectly straight nose. In front of a large crowd in the marketplace, Rahil took Gaitha's hand in his, and sang:

Goat Girl, oh Goat Girl,
For you I do yearn!
So Goat Girl, oh Goat Girl,
My heart do not spurn!

Once more, the people in the marketplace giggled among themselves, keenly anticipating Gaitha's joy and subsequent rejection, but once more, Gaitha was unmoved:

Suitor, oh Suitor,
You can't have my hand,
For Suitor, oh suitor,
Your toes are too fanned!

Rahil looked down at his feet, and felt his eyes blur with tears; he had always been self-conscious about the large gaps between his toes, but because he was handsome he thought nobody had noticed them. He ran from the marketplace, his face red with humiliation, and Gaitha shrugged and carried on with her day.

The villagers, meanwhile, were now furious their teasing had backfired all over again. It was beyond them how someone as ugly as Gaitha could be so choosy, and they were determined to punish her for her pride. So they sent word to the nearest town, and convinced a man even handsomer than Zaman and Rahil to present himself to the Goat Girl and declare his love, so after she had fallen for him, they could all laugh at her foolishness.

This youth was called Mujdi, and he was indeed very attractive, with big muscles, bright green eyes and, most importantly, a perfectly straight nose and perfectly normal toes. In front of a large crowd in the marketplace, Mujdi dropped to his knees in front of Gaitha, presented her with a ring, and sang:

Goat Girl, oh Goat Girl,
My soul is in strife!
So Goat Girl, oh Goat Girl,
You must be my wife!

But Gaitha took one look at the kneeling man, and sang:

Suitor, oh Suitor,
I can't be your bride,
For Suitor, oh suitor,
Your neck is too wide!

Mujdi gasped and hung his head; he had always been self-conscious about his thick neck, but because he was handsome he thought nobody had noticed it. He sped from the marketplace, his face hot with shame, and Gaitha shrugged and carried on with her day.

After this third incident, Gaitha's fame began to grow, and men would travel from all over the land to see quite how ugly she was in person, and they would take great pleasure in hearing themselves described by her sharp tongue. What had started as a nasty plot to demean her had turned into a cheerful game of insults, and large crowds would gather to watch the Goat Girl ridicule the appearance of whoever her latest suitor happened to be.

In fact, Gaitha was so well-known that even the prince had heard of her, and to amuse himself he invited her to the palace to insult all of his friends. Gaitha duly arrived and began to reel off their physical flaws one by one, and the prince, whose name was Nafiz, was delighted by her piercing wit.

'Will you insult me too, Gaitha?' he asked, deliberately not calling her by her cruel nickname.

Gaitha hesitated: she would have happily insulted any man, only she was aware that Nafiz, as a prince, was far from ordinary.

'Go on,' he urged her. 'Do your worst.'

Gaitha folded her arms:

You think I'll go easy, because you're a prince,
But I'll say quite plainly: your face make me wince.
I wish I'd not spent all that time on the road
To get to a palace ruled o'er by a toad.
Your hair is too tangled, your body too tall,
Your eyes are so vacant you could be a mule.
And really, your highness, you do make me squirm,
Your skin is so clammy you must be part worm.

Shall I keep speaking? I could talk all night,
And three days thereafter, you look such a fright.

As Gaitha paused, she realised the throne room had fallen into silence: clearly, nobody had ever dared to insult Prince Nafiz before, at least not to this extent. What would happen to her now? Could she be arrested for treason? Might she be imprisoned, or even executed?

But, to her great relief, the quiet was suddenly broken by the prince bursting into laughter. The sound of his mirth echoed around the throne room, and he laughed and laughed until tears were running down his cheeks.

'Very good,' he said, clapping his hands together. 'Now, I think it my turn.'

Gaitha was surprised and a little impressed that he had not run away or lost his temper or dissolved into tears, like all of her other faux-suitors.

'Go on, then,' she urged him. 'Do your worst.'

Prince Nafiz folded his arms:

Oh Gaitha, oh Gaitha, the girl they call goat,
You come to my palace with bile in your throat,
With words so insulting I should be quite sore,
But no, I just sit back and want to hear more.
You may not be pretty, you may not be fair,
Yet I think there's something about you quite rare :
You're clever, you're crafty, your insults disarm,

And that's more exciting than beauty and charm.
So Gaitha, oh Gaitha, it would be amiss,
To let you depart here devoid of my kiss.

And before Gaitha could prepare herself, Prince Nafiz had risen from his throne, taken her in his arms, and kissed her. For a moment, her heart leapt in her chest, but then she came to her senses, and she pushed the prince away.

'You are mocking me,' she said.

'I am not,' replied Nafiz, leaning in for another kiss.

But this time she ducked him. 'I am not stupid,' she said. 'I know you think it is funny to kiss an ugly girl like me! Later, you will laugh about my squint, my wonky teeth, my hairy chin...'

'If I do, you may laugh about my vacant mule eyes, my clammy worm skin, and you may giggle to your heart's content about your prince who looks like a toad,' said Nafiz.

Gaitha stared up at him: she could not think why she had said all of those horrible things. Now, no matter how much she scrutinised his appearance, she thought him perfect to look at, and her heart swelled with love.

They were married the next day. At first, there was a great deal of consternation over why the prince had chosen a girl who resembled a goat to be his bride, although most people were soon won over by Gaitha's spirit and wit. Her sharp tongue softened over the years, as nobody dared to make fun of a princess – at least, not to her face – and she was happy with the prince, whose intellect and humour matched her own. Moreover, although

Nafiz declared he did not care whether their children were the ugliest children in all of the land, Gaitha was secretly very relieved when she gave birth to a baby girl who had quite clearly inherited the looks of her father, the prince.

The Beggar's Coat

Once, there lived a beggar called Osnayan, although he was generally known throughout his village simply as 'Yan'. He had a noble face, a dark beard, and magnificent red *babouche* slippers that pointed at the toes. But the most striking thing about Osnayan's appearance was his big white coat, which was so long it covered his baggy *sirwal* and its hem dragged along the ground.

As far as anybody knew, Osnayan had no home, no family and no profession, and therefore he could often be found standing outside the mosque or the market, holding his hands in the sleeves of his large coat like an imam. Because he was always quiet and respectful, and because he possessed an aura of piety and dignity, his fellow villagers were charitable towards him, and would often press bread, fruit, vegetables and nuts into his arms, so Osnayan would never go hungry.

In this village, there also lived a bright young boy named Remy, who came from a good and relatively wealthy family. One day, as Remy was passing Osnayan in his usual spot in the marketplace, the boy offered the beggar man a copper coin from his pocket money.

'I am grateful to you, young man,' said Osnayan, 'but I have no need of money.'

He tried to hand it back to the boy, but Remy shook his head.

'It is for you, Yan,' he said. 'So you may buy food or shelter, or perhaps a new coat.'

'I have all the food and shelter I require,' said Osnayan, before adding with a wink, 'and I like my coat as it is. But I see this was kindly meant, so I will keep your coin.'

After this exchange, Remy grew curious about the serious man who stood so still and so silently outside the mosque and in the marketplace, relying on other people's handouts. Who was he? Where did he sleep? Did he have any clothes, other than those bright slippers and the long coat? After asking his parents and their friends, Remy was forced to conclude that nobody really knew very much at all about Osnayan.

Nevertheless, every time he received his pocket money, Remy would give Osnayan a little of it, and as the years passed and Remy started work, one copper coin turned into three silver ones. But although the amount Remy pushed into the beggar man's hands had changed, Osnayan's response remained the same: 'I am grateful to you, young man, but I have no need of money.'

'It is for you, Yan,' Remy said, over and over again. 'So you may buy food or shelter, or perhaps a new coat.'

But, as ever, Osnayan, replied, 'I have all the food and shelter I require, and I like my coat as it is. But I see this was kindly meant, so I will keep your coins.'

These words were almost always the same, but Remy grew more and more puzzled by them as he grew older, and began to set great store by money. He assumed Osnayan spent the scant coins he was given on food and shelter, because the beggar man had certainly not bought new clothes: his long white coat was now discoloured, frayed and covered in a dozen or so patches.

But Osnayan still seemed calm and content with his lot, and he remained a familiar and well-regarded figure around the village.

Around seven years after Remy had first pressed a coin upon Osnayan, the boy – who was now a man – made plans to leave his village and seek his fortune overseas. Before he left, he went to see the beggar man, and after he had entreated him to take three more silver coins, and following their usual conversation, Remy told his older friend of his plans.

'I wish you good luck, young man,' said Osnayan, 'and I hope, when you do make your fortune, you remember there is more to life than gold.'

Remy nodded politely and bade Osnayan goodbye, but now he was older he could see how different he was to this person who had never aspired to rise above the poverty into which he had been born, and so the young man felt he had no need for this advice.

Remy stayed away from his home village for many years, during which, because he was bright, he became a very rich man. When he finally returned to see his family, he also stopped by to check on Osnayan, who was still standing at his favourite spot in the market place. Seven more years had passed since Remy and Osnayan had last seen one another, and the beggar's hair and beard were now grey. Yet his clothes were the same, although his slippers were faded and his coat was dirty and covered in more patches than ever.

'Yan, you must take my money now,' said Remy, offering his old friend a whole bag of gold coins. 'You must buy food and shelter now you are older – and surely you are not so attached to that threadbare old coat. Please, take it: I am so rich, this money is nothing to me now.'

But Osnayan smiled and said, as he always did, 'I have all the food and shelter I require, and I like my coat as it is. But I see this was kindly meant, so I will keep your coins.'

Remy shook his head in disbelief, but he had known Osnayan too long to expect anything different. Then, not a few days later, he left the village again, to continue making his fortune overseas.

But this time, Remy was not so lucky. He became overconfident with his money, and placed his trust in the wrong people, until his wealth began to trickle away. By the time another seven years had passed, Remy had lost all of the money he had earned during his adult life, and he returned to his village a broken man.

While his family strove to comfort him, Remy could only think of Osnayan.

'How is my old friend?' he asked his mother. 'I have not seen him in the market place since I have been back.'

'He has not been there for many weeks,' she replied. 'Nobody knows where Old Yan has gone.'

This news roused Remy from his self-pity. He decided to search for his friend, and after he had asked many of the market stallholders whether they had seen Osnayan, he was directed to a place by the river, just on the outskirts of the village. There, he found a shabby old tent, and around it a little vegetable patch, a barbecue, and even some fishing tackle. Remy then entered the tent, and found Osnayan lying upon an old mattress and tatty blankets. The beggar was very old now; his face was lined and his hair was as white as snow. For once, he wasn't wearing his slippers or coat, and Remy thought this made him look especially small in his bed.

'Yan!' cried Remy, in alarm. 'Yan, are you ill?'

'I am dying, my boy,' said Osnayan, 'but do not look so sad about it: I have had a very good life.'

'But how can you say that when you have been so poor!' replied Remy.

This time, it was Osnayan who shook his head. 'You still do not understand, do you? I have been the wealthiest man in all of the village. I have lived off the land, as you see outside, and I have relied on the kindness of my friends – friends like you.'

Remy thought about this, and wondered whether Osnayan might be right: although he had acquired a huge amount of money over the years, it had never made him particularly happy.

'Perhaps I would have been better if I had lived like you,' said Remy, before telling Osnayan about his misfortune. 'If I had lived a humbler life, I would not be so devastated by the loss of my gold.'

Osnayan smiled. 'Remy, because you have been so generous to me over the years, I would like to give you a gift,' he said.

Remy looked around the shabby tent at Osnayan's scant belongings: what did the man have to give him? A few leftover nuts from the market? Some dried fish? A rusty old lantern from his tent?

'It is as you always tell me, Yan,' he said, 'I do not need any more possessions.'

'Ah, but this is my favourite possession, and so I want it to go to you. Remy, I wish to give you my coat.'

'Your coat?' Remy tried to disguise his disappointment. Osnayan's old coat, which was hanging on the wall, was now a pitiful object: it was still big – in fact it looked bigger than ever – but it was now so dirty, worn, and covered in so many patches, it was impossible to tell it had once been a smart white coat. But then, as Osnayan had told him so many times before, the offer was kindly meant, so Remy took the coat off the hook and bade Osnayan goodbye one last time.

A few days later, the villagers learned that Osnayan the beggar had died. Although it was said the old man had passed away peacefully in his sleep, Remy was grief-stricken at the news. It seemed too much to bear, especially after the loss of his savings and his own personal crisis.

While he mourned in his old bedroom, Remy decided to honour his friend Yan by putting on his famous coat. But as he slipped the grubby garment over his shoulders, he was surprised by the weight of it: Remy had not noticed this before, when carrying it after leaving Osnayan, although perhaps that was because his heart had been heavy too. But now he was bewildered by the way the coat pulled down on his shoulders and, stranger still, when he paced about his room, the material made a clinking sound as it moved.

Frowning, Remy checked the pockets of the coat, and found them empty. Then his fingers brushed against something hard under one of the patches, and he pulled at the thread around it until the object toppled out: it was a copper coin, exactly like the ones he had given Osnayan as a boy. With an effort, Remy shrugged the coat from his shoulders, and began to unpick the patches one by one. More coins fell out – copper, silver and even gold – until, an hour later, Remy had made a pile of money in the corner of his bedroom. This, he knew, was everything he had given Osnayan over the years, from his pocket money all those years ago, to the bag of gold when he had been a rich man. And Osnayan had kept every coin.

'So Yan really did have no need of my money after all,' said Remy, as he stared at the heap of wealth in the corner. 'Yet still he held onto it. I wonder if he knew I would need it back some day?'

Though he could not be sure, Remy thought he knew the answer to this question. He gathered up the coins and counted them, and because many years had passed since he had started giving money to Osnayan, the copper, silver and gold was worth far more than it had been back then, and Remy was a rich man once again. Yet he reminded himself of Osnayan's final words to him: *I have been the wealthiest man in all of the village. I have lived off the land... and I have relied on the kindness of my friends – friends like you.* Reflecting on this wisdom, Remy pledged to place less importance on wealth. With Osnayan's gold, he bought himself a little farm outside the village, and there he lived a humbler life, and always spared a coin or two for any beggar he encountered.

The Fox's Tail

Once upon a time, there was a little old lady who lived on her own. Yet despite being a widow, and almost eighty years old, she was a healthy, active woman, who could often be seen bustling about the town. Whenever people asked the old woman how she stayed so spritely, she would always reply, 'Every morning, I get up early and milk my goat. Then I drink half a pail of that milk in the morning, and half a pail of that milk in the afternoon, and that is what keeps me in fine fettle.'

But one day, after the woman had returned from the market, she discovered that the half pail of milk she had left on the windowsill for the afternoon was gone. The bucket was still there, but it was now completely empty, as though someone had licked it clean. The old lady scratched at her head, wondering what could have happened: she had definitely left half a pail's worth of milk there, and she had no children or family living with her, so there was nobody in the house who could have drunk it. It was quite a mystery, especially when the same thing happened the next day, and that afternoon's milk disappeared too.

On the third day, the woman decided to take action. She left the half a pail of milk on the windowsill as usual, but instead of going to market, she hid behind the curtain to wait for the thief. Sure enough, after a half an hour or so, the door creaked open, and a fox with a magnificent bushy tail snuck into her house. He slunk towards the windowsill, stood up on his hind legs, and began to slurp at the milk.

'Oh ho!' cried the woman, leaping out from behind the curtain. 'Thief!'

The fox froze, milk dripping from his muzzle and whiskers, and then made to bolt out of the house. But the woman gave chase, and tried to close the door so he couldn't escape. The fox just managed to slip out, but his tail was caught as she slammed the door shut, and it came clean off, flopping to the floor like a duster.

'Oh well,' said the woman, picking it up, 'at least I tracked down the thief. I may not have been able to give him a piece of my mind, but it seems he gave me a piece of himself instead, so I shall place this magnificent red tail on my mantelpiece to put off any future thieves.'

The next day, however, she was very surprised to discover the fox knocking at her door. He looked very small and pitiful without his beautiful tail, and he seemed to know it, for great tears were dripping down his furry cheeks.

'Please, lady, may I have my tail back?' he said. 'I look like a little rat without it, and the other animals make fun of me. Plus, no vixen will look twice at me without a tail. Please, won't you give it back?'

But the old woman frowned. 'You are a little thief,' she said.

'I know, I am very sorry I drank your milk!' sobbed the fox.

'You are only sorry because you have been caught,' she said. 'No, Mr Fox, you took something from me, so I think it right I take something from you. I will keep your tail, which I think looks very fine on my mantelpiece.'

'No!' cried the fox. 'Please, no! I will do anything!'

The old lady folded her arms. She was not without pity, and the fox really did look a pathetic sight without his tail.

'All right,' she said, 'if you can replace the two portions of milk you drank – that's a full pail, mind – you may have your tail back.'

'Oh thank you, thank you!'

'But be warned,' said the old woman, 'my goat is a cantankerous creature, and she won't give her milk to just anyone.'

But the fox was already skipping away, determined to fulfil this task and get back his tail.

The goat, who was tied up in the yard, snorted with laughter as the fox came into view, for he did look very strange. But the fox ignored her, and instead cleared his throat and said:

I need your milk, oh, just one pail,
In order to reclaim my tail.

The goat chewed on her leaves for a while, thinking this over. Then she said, 'You are not my mistress. If I give you a pail of milk, what will you give me in return?'

'Anything you like,' replied the fox.

The goat spat out her mouthful of leaves and said, 'I am sick of these old leaves. I would like leaves from the mulberry tree instead, they are far sweeter. If you fetch me ten leaves from the mulberry tree, I will give you a pail of milk.'

So the fox skidded off towards the nearest mulberry tree, which also laughed at his peculiar appearance, but the fox ignored it and said:

I need ten leaves plucked from your tree,
A goat would like them for her tea.
I need her milk, oh, just one pail,
In order to reclaim my tail.

The mulberry tree, which was drifting back and forth in the breeze, thought this over. Then it said, 'I do not belong to you. If I give you ten leaves from my tree, what will you give me in return?'

'Anything you like,' replied the fox.

The mulberry tree looked down at the ground, which was very dry and cracked, and said, 'I cannot grow in this parched earth. If you fetch me some water from the river, I will give you ten leaves from my tree.'

So the fox dashed off towards the nearest river, which also chuckled at his odd appearance, but the fox ignored it and said:

I need some water from your flow,
To help a mulberry tree to grow.
I need ten leaves plucked from its tree,
A goat would like them for her tea.
I need her milk, oh, just one pail,
In order to reclaim my tail.

The river thought this over as it drifted alongside the bank. Then it said, 'I belong to no one. If I give you water from my flow, what will you give me in return?'

'Anything you like,' replied the fox.

The river looked up at the bank on either side of its body and said, 'I am not as deep and full as I once was. If you go to the clouds and encourage them to rain, then I will be able to give you some water from my flow.'

So the fox sped up to the top of a mountain, where he was high enough to speak to the clouds. They also rumbled with laughter at his bizarre appearance, but the fox ignored them and said:

> *I need you to turn dark and rain,*
> *To make the river whole again*
> *I need some water from its flow,*
> *To help a mulberry tree to grow.*
> *I need ten leaves plucked from its tree,*
> *A goat would like them for her tea.*
> *I need her milk, oh, just one pail,*
> *In order to reclaim my tail.*

The clouds talked this over among themselves for a few moments. Then they said, 'We like staying white and fluffy, not turning dark. If we rain, what will you give us in return?'

'Anything you like,' replied the fox.

The clouds peered down at the earth and said, 'We only like to rain when we are encouraged. If you go to the town, there are three female dancers we like very much. If they perform for us, we will turn dark and rain.'

So the fox hurried back down the mountain, and into the town, where he found the three female dancers lounging idly in the market place. They giggled at his comical appearance, but the fox ignored them and said:

I need you to perform your dance,
To put the clouds into a trance.
I need them to turn dark and rain,
To make the river whole again.
I need some water from its flow,
To help a mulberry tree to grow.
I need ten leaves plucked from its tree,
A goat would like them for her tea.
I need her milk, oh, just one pail,
In order to reclaim my tail.

The dancers whispered to one another for a little while. Then the most beautiful of the three spoke in a high voice, 'It is our day off, and we were hoping to remain here in the market place. If we dance, what will you give us in return?'

'Anything you like,' replied the fox.

The women looked down at their shoes, which were very old and worn, and said, 'We would like new shoes. These ones are falling apart. If you get us new shoes, we will dance for the clouds.'

So the fox hurried through the town to the cobbler, who chortled at his unusual look, but the fox ignored him and said:

I need six shoes, both smart and neat,
To fit three female dancers' feet.
I need them to perform their dance,
To put the clouds into a trance.
I need them to turn dark and rain,
To make the river whole again.
I need some water from its flow,
To help a mulberry tree to grow.
I need ten leaves plucked from its tree,
A goat would like them for her tea.
I need her milk, oh, just one pail,
In order to reclaim my tail.

The cobbler scratched at his long white beard and said, 'Six is a lot of shoes. If I make these three pairs for you, what will you give me in return?'

'Anything you like,' replied the fox.

The cobbler clutched at his stomach, which was growling in hunger, and said, 'Every morning, I sit in my workshop and I am so hungry, because I do not have eggs for my breakfast. If you can fetch me a dozen eggs – two for each shoe – I will craft this footwear for these dancers.'

So the fox slipped out of the town and towards the nearest farm, where he crawled into the henhouse. The hen he found there did not laugh at his lack of tail, because although he looked ridiculous, she could still tell he was a dangerous fox. For his part, the fox was just as hungry as the cobbler had been, having run hither and thither on his quest, and he was tempted to gobble up the hen there and then. But he knew he would not retrieve his tail that way, and so he ignored his hunger and said:

I need your eggs, twelve at least,
The cobbler wants a morning feast.
I need his shoes, both smart and neat,
To fit three female dancers' feet.
I need them to perform their dance,
To put the clouds into a trance.
I need them to turn dark and rain,
To make the river whole again
I need some water from its flow,
To help a mulberry tree to grow.
I need ten leaves plucked from its tree,
A goat would like them for her tea.
I need her milk, oh, just one pail,
In order to reclaim my tail.

The hen wriggled on her nest and said, 'You are not my farmer. If I lay these eggs for you, what will you give me in return?'

'I will promise not to eat you,' growled the fox.

But the hen stood her ground. 'If you eat me, you will not get any eggs at all,' she said. 'So tell me, what will you give me in return?'

The fox sighed. 'Anything you like,' he replied.

The hen gave this some thought. 'Twelve is a lot of eggs,' she said. 'In order for me to lay that many, I will need an extra scoop of corn. If you can convince the farmer's wife to give me twice as much corn, you may have your eggs.'

So the fox trotted from the henhouse and towards the farm, where he found the farmer's wife in the kitchen. She did not laugh at his appearance either, for she was rocking a crying babe in her arms, and the fox had to speak very loudly to be heard above the noise:

I need some corn, an extra scoop,
To feed a hen in your coop.
I need her eggs, twelve at least,
The cobbler wants a morning feast.
I need his shoes, both smart and neat,
To fit three female dancers' feet.
I need them to perform their dance,
To put the clouds into a trance.
I need them to turn dark and rain,
To make the river whole again.
I need some water from its flow,
To help a mulberry tree to grow.
I need ten leaves plucked from its tree,
A goat would like them for her tea.
I need her milk, oh, just one pail,
In order to reclaim my tail.

'Goodness,' said the farmer's wife, 'you need a lot of things, don't you?'

The fox nodded miserably. He was beginning to feel exhausted.

'If you give me the corn, I will give you anything in return,' he said, anticipating her question.

'All I want is some peace,' admitted the farmer's wife, for the child was still bawling in her arms. 'Look, little fox, if you watch my daughter, I would be glad to go to the storehouse and give the hens an extra scoop of corn. A few moments of quiet are all *I* need.'

The fox agreed to this deal at once, and after the farmer's wife had set off, he looked at the squalling baby she had left behind. By now, he was very hungry indeed, and was tempted to gobble up the child, as he had been tempted to gobble up the hen. But the fox reminded himself that the farmer's wife was unlikely to take kindly to him and give the hens more corn if he ate her baby, and the last time he had stolen food it had lost him his tail. So instead, because his ears were ringing from the noise, the fox attempted to soothe the crying child. He prodded the baby with his paws and tickled her with his whiskers until she giggled, and then she snuggled against his soft fur and fell asleep. Yawning widely, the fox put the thought of eating her from his mind once more, and he too began to snooze.

Sometime later, he was woken by the farmer's wife, who was almost crying herself with gratitude.

'You dear, dear creature!' she whispered. 'I cannot thank you enough for getting my baby to sleep. I have given the hens a very large scoop of extra corn.'

Suddenly awake, the fox leapt up, his heart full of hope. 'Now, at last, I can reclaim my tail!' he said.

The following afternoon, while the old woman was drinking her usual half a pail of milk, there was a knock at her door.

'Who could that be?' she said to herself, shuffling across the room to open it.

She was somewhat surprised to find the thieving fox on her doorstep, who still looked absurd without his tail.

'You were gone so long, I didn't think you were coming back,' she said. 'Tell me, Mr Fox, did you convince the goat to give you a pail of milk.'

The fox took a deep breath, and said:

I caused a baby's cries to cease,
To give a farmer's wife some peace.
She fetched some corn, an extra scoop,
To feed a hen in her coop.
The hen laid eggs, twelve at least,
Fit for a cobbler's morning feast.
He made six shoes, both smart and neat,
To fit three female dancers' feet.
They climbed up high, performed their dance,
And put the clouds into a trance.
The sky, it then began to rain,
And made the river whole again.
I took some water from its flow,
To help a mulberry tree to grow.

It gave me ten leaves from its tree,
Your goat desired them for her tea.
And now I've milk – at last, one pail!
So please, will you return my tail?

And with that, the fox triumphantly reached behind his back and held up a bucket, full to the brim with goat's milk.

'Well!' said the old lady, after inspecting the contents of the pail. 'You have been on an adventure, haven't you, Mr Fox? I didn't know I had set you such a task. But of course, I will keep my word and give you back your tail, even though I think it looks very fine on my mantelpiece.'

While the fox danced with joy, she reached up for the bushy red tail, and then she fetched a needle and thread and sewed it back on for him, although he was so excited she had to tell him several times to sit still. After that, the old lady and the fox became friends, and every so often he would call round to keep her company. Sometimes, she would even let him have a few sips of her goat's milk, although he had learned from experience to never again take any without asking.

The Prince and his Horse

Once, far away, a whole kingdom went into mourning, for their beautiful young queen had fallen very ill and died. No one was more upset by this tragedy than her only son, Prince Roy, who thought he would never recover from the loss of his mother.

'I cannot bear to see my boy so sad,' sighed the grieving king to himself. 'I must try to distract him from his melancholy, I must arrange for a gift that will bring some light and laughter back into his life.'

He talked the matter over with his vizier and they agreed that the best course of action was to buy Prince Roy a young horse. Then, not only could the boy learn to ride, he could also care for this animal, which might in turn offer him some comfort in the wake of his mother's death.

So the purchase was arranged, and the next day a beautiful white Arabian horse of two years old was delivered to the palace. As the king had hoped, Prince Roy was delighted with the creature, which ran and jumped merrily about the grounds, bringing joy to all who saw it.

'There,' said the king, watching his son smile for the first time in many months. 'I think he will emerge from his grief now, as he masters this horse.'

But this was not exactly the case, for while Prince Roy was indeed greatly cheered by his colt, the relationship between them was never one of master and dumb beast. On the contrary, from that first day, the horse became the prince's constant companion, and there developed a bond between them so strong that the boy began to think of the animal like a kind of brother.

Perhaps due to this bond – or maybe there was a kind of magic in their meeting – Prince Roy soon found that he could communicate with his horse. Not in words, exactly, as the animal had none, but it was almost as though they could read one another's thoughts, and eventually they could have whole conversations about the weather, about where they were to ride that day, or even about the palace gossip. Yet something told the Prince that he would do well to keep this secret, so while everyone knew how deeply he cared for the colt, nobody had any idea the pair of them could communicate.

So the years went by and though both Prince Roy and the colt grew up, almost to adulthood, their bond remained ever unbreakable. The king, however, with no such companion, began to feel very lonely, and his vizier recommended that it was time to find another wife.

Unfortunately, the woman he chose had the opposite temperament to his first, sweet wife. The new queen was cold and cruel, and only interested in the king for the power of his position. She also hated Prince Roy, for she knew that he was first in the line of succession, ahead of any children she might have.

As time wore on, the queen's hatred for her stepson grew and grew. Then, when she fell pregnant, she decided she could bear it no longer : she would have Prince Roy murdered, making his death look like an accident, and then her child would be the sole heir to the throne.

To carry out this task, the wicked queen enlisted the help of one of the palace guards, a big brute of a man whom she often took to her bed. The pair met under cover of darkness to discuss her villainous intentions.

'Take this, it is filled with poison,' the queen told the guard, handing him a small glass vial. 'Slip a few drops into the young prince's food tomorrow night and he will not live to see another day.'

Then she departed, confident that her plan would be a success.

Fortunately for the prince, however, the queen and the guard had had this conversation within earshot of the stables, and the prince's horse had overheard everything. So the next day, when he was galloping around the countryside with the young royal on his back, the horse issued a grave warning.

Your stepmother intends to poison you, he told Prince Roy, in that strange way of speaking that they had. *You must not eat any of your food tonight. In fact, if you are handed a plate, you must throw it away, so it will not harm anyone else by accident. Do you understand?*

The prince, ruffling his beloved horse's mane said, 'Yes, I understand. Thank you, my friend.'

So that evening, as the queen intended, the guard laced Prince Roy's food with poison before it was taken to the main table. But the prince, heeding his horse's warning, did not eat a bite. Instead, he stood up, strode over to the window, and threw his plate and all of its contents into the night.

'Son!' the king cried, shocked by this display of bad manners. 'What is the meaning of this!'

'Sorry, father, I just did not feel very hungry tonight.'

Nervously, all of the courtiers began to laugh, as though they all thought the prince was trying to make a joke. The queen, however, did not even smile – instead she glowered all the way through the meal and then, when the dining was done, hurried back outside to meet the guard.

'He knew!' she hissed. 'I don't know how, but he knew it was poisoned! Curse him!'

She paced up and down in front of the stables while the guard watched her, blinking stupidly.

'We must try again,' muttered the queen eventually. 'Do you still have that vial I gave you?'

The guard nodded.

'Good. Tomorrow, take some needles, dip them in that poison, and scatter them in front of his chambers. Then, when the prince is heading to bed, they will pierce his feet and he will fall into an eternal sleep!'

Yet despite her confidence in this new plan, once more she had spoken of it in front of the stables, and once more Prince Roy's beloved horse had overheard everything. So the next day, when he was jumping over hedges with the young royal on his back, the horse issued a second grave warning.

Your stepmother intends to attempt your life again, he told the prince. *Only this time, she will place poisoned needles outside your chambers. You must not step over them on your way to bed tonight, instead you must jump as far and as high as you can – like me, do you see?*

To demonstrate, the horse leapt over a deep ditch. When he landed, the prince patted him on the neck. 'Yes, I see. Thank you, my friend.'

So, once more, Prince Roy evaded death by jumping over the poisoned needles, and when his stepmother saw him alive and well at breakfast the next day, she was filled with disbelief and rage. This time, she summoned the guard directly to her chambers.

'He knew again!' she hissed. 'How did he know? No one could have heard us plotting, unless…' She paused, thinking of their previous proximity to the stables. 'Unless it was that wretched horse of his that warned him…'

'But horses don't talk,' the guard pointed out.

'I know that, fool!' she snapped. 'But the bond between that boy and that horse is unusual – unnatural, even. The creature warned him somehow, it's the only way he could have known.'

'So shall we try again?' the guard asked.

But the queen shook her head, a cruel smile playing about her lips. 'No. Let us first remove the horse from the situation, and then we will deal with the prince. The delay is unfortunate,' she said, rubbing at her pregnant belly, 'but the death of the boy's favourite beast will cause him great suffering, which will in turn amuse me.'

So together, the queen and the guard began to concoct a heinous plan. She would pretend to be taken ill, and they would bribe a doctor to declare that she and her unborn child would surely die if she did not receive some special medicine immediately: the blood of a thoroughbred, white Arabian horse. The king, despite knowing how much Prince Roy's horse meant to him, would nevertheless order the slaughter of the animal, for he would be so afraid that his second wife – and their baby – would meet the same fate as his first.

No sooner had she worked out these details, the queen began the charade of falling ill and, as planned, the dishonest doctor proclaimed that only the blood of a thoroughbred, white Arabian horse would save her. So, with a heavy heart, the king went out to the grounds to where his son was cantering about on his favourite steed and explained what had to be done.

The queen is pretending, the horse told Prince Roy. *She is trying to dispose of me to get at you. She is not ill at all.*

But the young royal had worked this out on his own, for he now knew only too well the ruthless character of his stepmother.

'Father, I will do as you say,' he said, arranging his face into a solemn expression, 'but first, let me ride my horse once around the castle grounds – to say goodbye. You will grant me that at least?'

The king sighed, but found he could not refuse his son this one thing. 'Go then,' he said, 'but return as quickly as you can. The doctor said we must drain the animal's blood at the earliest opportunity.'

The prince nodded, leaned forward and whispered in the horse's ear, 'Run! Run, boy, run!'

But the horse was already setting off, speeding up to full pelt, galloping so wildly that the young prince had to hold on tightly in order to stay on his back. And, to the king's surprise and horror, they did not stop when they reached the boundary of the castle grounds, but took a great leap over the wall, laughing and whinnying as the wind whipped at their faces. On and on they sped, through villages and towns, beside streams and rivers, through fields and deserts, and over hills and mountains, until the palace was no longer even a speck on the horizon. After three days of galloping, they had crossed into the next kingdom and, exhausted, Prince Roy slid off his horse's back.

'There now,' he said, stroking the animal's furry nose. 'We will be safe from my stepmother here.'

Once they had rested, the prince and his horse considered what they were going to do, now that they had forsaken their old, comfortable life in the other kingdom. They were both still young and yearned to explore, but Prince Roy was aware that now, with no title or fortune to speak of, he would have to find a way to make a living. Reluctant to tie his horse to a life of drudgery, he removed the saddle from the animal's back and the bridle from his head.

'It looks as though the time has come for us to part, my friend,' he said sadly.

Perhaps, replied the horse, *but if you should ever need me, I will be there. Pluck three strands of hair from my tail and keep them close. Then, if ever you should find yourself in want of aid, burn one of the hairs and I will come running. Do you understand?*

'I understand,' said the former prince, taking three hairs from the horse's tail before wrapping his arms around the animal's neck as they wished one another farewell.

Given that he had been raised as royalty, young Roy was not skilled in any profession, so he had to give some thought as to what he wanted to do now that he had gone from riches to rags. He had always enjoyed spending time outside, especially with his horse, and he thought that he might like to become a gardener. So that is exactly what he did, and it turned out that the prince had a good understanding of how to care for plants, flowers, vegetables and fruits. Within a year, he was much in demand, so much so that he was given a job as one of the royal gardeners, where he came to spend his days tending the lawns and flowerbeds of the palace in his new home kingdom.

It happened to be that the ruler of this kingdom had three daughters, and some of the gardens for which Roy was responsible were directly underneath the middle daughter's balcony. So when the young and beautiful princess, whose name was Averina, came outside to watch the sun rise or set, or to simply gaze at the moon and stars, Roy found himself falling deeply and desperately in love with her.

With no thought to his new social standing, Roy set about trying to woo her, arranging extravagant displays of flowers beneath her window in order to attract her attention. The princess, charmed by these floral tributes, quickly became intrigued by the handsome young gardener, who had curiously impeccable manners for one so low born. They began to converse in secret, she from the balcony and he from the garden, and within a few weeks Princess Averina was just as in love with Roy as he was with her.

'But, though it breaks my heart to say it, we cannot be together,' she whispered sadly. 'For my older sister is not wed, and my father, the king, will not allow me to marry before her!'

Upon hearing this, Roy was distraught, and could not think of who to turn to for advice or solace. Then, remembering his horse's words – *if you should ever need me, I will be there* – he took out one of the three silvery white hairs that he always carried around inside his pocket and burnt it. As the hair curled into nothingness in the flame, Roy called softly for help:

I need your aid, my loyal steed,
So hurry, friend, to me now speed.

A few moments later, as though by magic, the white horse was by his side. Overjoyed to see his old friend, Roy patted his back and ruffled his mane, before he grew serious, remembering his predicament.

'Friend, I want to marry Princess Averina, but her father won't let her wed until her older sister is married. What shall I do?'

The horse considered this and then said, *Collect three apples from the garden: one that is old and rotten, one that is sour and unripe, and one that is just right. Then leave them in the king's throne room, and I think your problem will be solved.*

The prince did not understand this instruction, but he trusted the horse above all others, so he did as the animal suggested. Then, after one joyful ride around the palace together, the pair parted ways once more.

The next day, when the king discovered the three apples in the throne room, he was greatly puzzled. He could not think how they had come to be there, yet they seemed significantly positioned in a line before his royal chair, so he wondered if they might be some sort of sign. With this in mind, he called for his advisor, the palace's guru, and asked him what he thought the apples meant.

'Hm, you were right to question this, my King,' said the guru, examining the line of fruit. 'And I think it is clear what God is telling us: the apples represent your daughters. The old and rotten apple is, I am afraid to say, your eldest daughter, as it is now too late for her to marry and bear children. The sour and unripe apple is, I believe, your youngest daughter, as she is not yet ready to marry and bear children.'

'But this is very bad news!' cried the king in panic. 'For who will continue the royal line?'

'Ah, but look at this apple,' said the guru, pointing at the one that was just right. 'It is rosy and ripe, and I think we are being told that your middle daughter, Averina, is ready to be married.'

When the king told Averina this news, she clapped her hands together with joy and said, 'Oh Father, I wish to marry Roy, one of the palace gardeners!'

But the king threw his head back with laughter. 'A gardener?' he roared. 'I would never allow a daughter of mine to marry a commoner! No, we will send out invitations to all of the princes in the neighbouring kingdoms, so that they might come and attempt to win your hand, my dear. A gardener, indeed!' he chuckled.

When Averina tearfully told him of this, Roy was very distressed. For he still thought of himself as a prince, so had overlooked how ill-matched he and the princess appeared to be. Humbly, he approached the king on bended knee and begged him to change his mind. And while the king was impressed by Roy's appearance and manners, he could not come to terms with his low social standing.

'Please, give me some hope!' Roy pleaded with him. 'What would you have me do?'

Not wishing to appear ungenerous, the king gave this some thought. What *did* he want? Unbeknownst to many of his subjects, he suffered from a great many minor ailments, though he tried not to let them show so as not to appear weak. But legend had it that there existed in his kingdom an animal whose blood contained remarkable healing properties…

'If you can hunt me a white gazelle,' said the king, 'you may have Princess Averina's hand in marriage.'

The courtiers all gasped at these words, for they too had heard that the blood of the white gazelle (unlike the blood of a white Arabian horse) was said to have fabulous healing powers. Only, no one knew this for sure, as no one had ever been fast enough to catch one of the animals before. The king had set Roy an impossible task.

Or was it? For, no sooner had the ruler made this promise than Roy burned the second hair from his horse's tail:

I need your aid, my loyal steed,
So hurry, friend, to me now speed.

Once more, as though by magic, the white horse appeared within moments at Roy's side.

'Friend, now the princess' father will let her marry, but not a commoner of the kind I am pretending to be, unless I can hunt down a white gazelle. What shall I do?'

The horse considered this and then said, *Ride upon my back and we will hunt down the white gazelle together. It is fast, but I will be faster. Then we will bring its body to the king, and I think your problem will be solved.*

So the pair of them set out together, cantering out into the desert plains of the kingdom until they spotted the elusive white gazelle. The creature dashed away as it saw them approach, but the horse gave chase, galloping faster than ever before, faster than Roy even thought possible. The pursuit lasted a long time, but eventually the white gazelle began to tire. Then, when its pace had slowed, Roy was able to raise his bow, aim, and fire an arrow directly into the creature's heart.

The king was so surprised and impressed when Roy subsequently returned to the palace with the body of the almost-mythical creature, he did not even object too much to keeping his promise. For, despite his common birth, it was clear that the young gardener was an exceptional huntsman, one who would hopefully father some strong heirs to the throne. And so, with the king's blessing, and without anyone ever knowing the truth of the gardener's position, Roy and Averina were married.

For many years, Roy was content. He lived in a beautiful palace, he had a lovely wife, and together they had three sweet children. Sometimes he thought fleetingly of his father and his home, but he had been pretending to be a lowly gardener for so long that sometimes he forgot about his true past.

This changed, however, when Averina's father received an ambassador at court one day.

'Your neighbour, the king, is very sick,' he reported. 'They are saying he is dying. His wife seems poised to put her young son on the throne, but the people do not trust her. There is unrest across the border.'

When Roy heard all of this, he felt very concerned and upset. Not only was he worried for his father's health, he also knew full well that the throne was his, not his half-brother's, and it was up to him to stop his stepmother's scheming. But how should he proceed?

Taking out the last of the silver white hairs, he threw it in the fire:

I need your aid, my loyal steed,
So hurry, friend, to me now speed.

It had been a long time now, since Roy had seen his beloved horse, so when the creature appeared at his side he gave a cry of joy.

'Oh, my old friend!' he said mournfully. 'Have you heard what is happening in my kingdom? My father is dying and my stepmother wants to rule through her young son. Why, she has probably poisoned him to hurry the succession along. Oh, what shall I do?'

The horse looked at Roy, his dark, intelligent gaze steady. *I think it is time we went home,* he told the prince. *I think then your problems will be solved.*

Roy knew that his friend was right, and that it was time to stop hiding from who he was, so the first step he took was to go to Averina and her father and tell them the truth. Although they were greatly surprised by his story, he was so dear to both of them that they believed him at once, and vowed to help him in any way they could.

So it was that the king gathered a great army with which to march on the neighbouring kingdom and confront the wicked queen. Roy, atop his faithful white steed, rode at the head, and when word reached his stepmother that he had returned, she came out to meet them.

'So, you are alive,' she sneered.

'As are you,' Roy noted. 'I was under the impression that only the blood of a white Arabian horse could save you from your illness, all those years ago.'

Under him, his horse grunted with dislike. The queen, however, ignored the both of them.

'I had rather hoped *you* had died after you ran off, but apparently not. Apparently, you now have *allies*.' She gestured towards the army at his back. 'But it is too late, your father is dying, and after he is gone my son will be king.'

'You are wrong on both counts,' said Roy.

Then, before she or her guards could stop them, he and his horse dashed forward, galloping through the palace gates and even into the main entrance hall so fast that nobody could stop them. Then Roy ran up the steps to his father's chamber, where he found the king just as gravely ill as the queen had claimed.

'Son? Is that really you?' he croaked.

'It is,' replied Roy, kneeling beside the bed. 'Father, I have returned.'

'You are almost too late, I am not long for this world.'

But Roy shook his head. 'No, I think you will rule for many years yet. You see, I have come to save you, father.'

And from his pocket, he withdrew a vial of the white gazelle's blood, which the neighbouring king had given him to save his father. Just as it worked on minor ailments, so it worked against poison.

Meanwhile, on Roy's orders, the army arrested the unpopular queen and all of her co-conspirators and threw them into the dungeons. Presently, Roy issued a royal pardon to his half-brother, who seemed to have inherited more of his father's gentle temperament than his mother's wicked one, but his treacherous stepmother he left in the coldest, darkest cell, and swore that she would never again see beyond those four walls.

Then, with the king restored, the queen disposed of, the lost prince returned, and two great kingdoms united by the marriage of Roy and Averina, there was great rejoicing throughout all of the land.

The Pickle Wife

There was once a young merchant who, despite being very rich and successful, was afraid of one thing: marriage. All of his friends were married, but the thought of finding a wife seemed such a daunting task that it made his teeth chatter and his knees knock together in fear.

The truth was, this merchant's life was probably a little too comfortable for his own good, for he still lived with his mother, and she doted upon him. She washed his clothes, she tidied his room and, most importantly, she cooked him the most extravagant and delicious meals, for she was by far the best cook in all of the town. Being cared for by his mother meant that there was nothing at all to trouble the young merchant outside of his work, and so he worried that a wife might upset his very pleasant and comfortable existence.

Yet as the years went on and the merchant grew older, it began to look a little odd that he was unmarried. Although he was slightly chubby as a result of his mother's cooking, he wasn't a bad-looking man, and his wealth made him an attractive prospective husband for the town's young ladies. Indeed, his lack of interest in courting any of them caused some gossips to wonder whether there was something the matter with him, for who would not want a nice young wife to keep one company?

Now the merchant did not care one jot what people were saying in the marketplace, but as his mother bought ingredients for her wonderful food there every day, she found she could not bear to hear people whispering about her son. So, although she would have liked to spoil and mollycoddle him forever, she realised that sooner or later he would have to grow up: he would have to find a wife.

That evening, over an exquisite dinner of lamb shish kebabs, she brought up the subject of marriage. Now, if anyone else had tried to start this conversation with the merchant, he would have cut them off before they had finished the first sentence, but he listened to his mother. And eventually, by the time they had finished the sweet baklava dessert, he was beginning to see sense.

'I suppose I will consider marriage,' he told her at last. 'But only if you can find me a woman who is kind, clever and beautiful – and you should be the one to look for her, Mother, as I do not trust anyone else with this task.'

This seemed a reasonable request to the well-meaning woman, and so she agreed to interview all of the eligible young maids in the village, in order to find a suitable match for the merchant.

'And remember!' he reminded her frequently, as she set off to see girl after girl after girl. 'She must be kind *and* clever *and* beautiful!'

A few weeks later, the merchant's mother came home with good news. Over a sumptuous feast of kibbe and stuffed vine leaves, she announced, 'Son, I believe I have found the wife for you. Her name is Kadija, and I am confident she will meet your high expectations.'

The merchant was immediately sceptical of this statement.

'Is Kadija kind?' he asked.

'Oh yes,' replied his mother. 'Kadija is one of the kindest girls in the town. She has a sweet and thoughtful temperament, and spends much of her spare time doing charity work.'

The merchant nodded: this sounded almost promising.

'But is Kadija clever?' he asked.

'Oh yes,' replied his mother once more. 'Kadija is probably the cleverest girl in the town. She is studying mathematics under some wonderful professors at the university, and spends six out of seven days at lectures, seminars and studying in the library.'

The merchant nodded again: this definitely sounded promising.

'Surely Kadija can't be beautiful as well?' he asked, for this seemed too much to hope for.

'But she is,' replied his mother. 'Kadija is certainly the most beautiful girl in the town. She has long, honey-coloured hair, green eyes, and a lovely figure. In fact, she has many suitors after her hand already, so I suggest we arrange a meeting quickly, my son.'

The merchant agreed, for despite his reluctance to marry, he had been rather beguiled by the sound of this girl, and so Kadija was invited to tea the following day. In person, she turned out to be just as kind, clever and beautiful as she had been described, as well as charming, witty and elegant. To the surprise of both his mother and himself, the merchant found himself falling easily in love with Kadija, and within a month the pair were married.

Yet, unfortunately for the merchant, married life turned out to be just as bothersome as he had feared. Kadija was indeed kind, and fussed over him when he returned from work; Kadija was indeed clever, and helped him with the accounting for his business; Kadija was indeed beautiful, and her beaming face made his heart leap in his chest. But the merchant had neglected to inform his mother of one more important condition for his wife-to-be: that she should be a good cook.

He discovered Kadija's lack of culinary prowess very early on. Having moved into a grand house together, they bade one another goodbye that morning, he heading to work and she heading to the university. All day long, the merchant smiled to himself, pleased that he had changed his mind about marriage, and eagerly anticipating seeing Kadija again that evening, and enjoying a delightful meal together. Yet when he returned to the house, he did not find shish kebabs or kibbe or even falafel on his plate: instead, he discovered a lone pickle, served with a measly smear of khardal mustard.

'Wh-what is this?' the merchant stammered, clutching at his rumbling stomach.

'A pickle, dear,' Kadija smiled. 'I do hope you enjoy it.'

He frowned. 'Is this everything there is to eat tonight?' he asked in horror.

Kadija nodded. 'I am afraid I am not a very good cook,' she confessed. 'I have spent so much time studying and doing charity work that I never learned my way around a kitchen. You do not mind, do you, my husband?'

And the merchant shook his head, for she was so kind, so clever and so beautiful that he did not think he could begrudge her her poor cooking skills. Then he ate the pathetic pickle and tried not to dwell on the hunger that he felt for the rest of the evening and into the night.

The next day, while going about his work, the merchant began to hope that the second meal Kadija served him would not be quite so bad as the first. Even if she were a terrible cook, perhaps she would be able to attempt a salad or even a sandwich. Yet once more, when he returned home that night, all that he found on his plate was a wretched pickle and a dollop of khardal mustard.

'Is this everything there is to eat tonight?' he asked again, with dread in his heart.

Kadija looked apologetic. 'I am afraid I am not a very good cook,' she said once more. 'You do not mind, do you, my husband?'

The merchant said nothing, unwilling to hurt her feelings, but after the third and fourth occasions on which he was served a pickle for dinner, he was starting to mind very much indeed. And when seven days had gone by, and he was beginning to feel weakened by his new diet, the merchant had had enough. That evening, he did not go home until very late: he simply could not face to look at another pickle, let alone eat one.

He considered going to his mother's house, for surely if she knew her son was going hungry she would cook a banquet for him. But he dismissed this idea, feeling it was disloyal to his wife to betray her to her mother-in-law. So instead the young merchant took to wandering the market, taking in the sights and smells of the kibbe, the spicy tanour bread with za'atar, the stuffed aubergine, the roast lamb, the shish kebabs. Yet however much his mouth watered and his stomach rumbled, he was too miserable to buy himself any dinner, and so instead he plonked himself down at the side of the street and begin to sing mournfully to himself:

I must lament my current strife,
This pain I'll bear no more.
You see, my kind and clever wife
Serves food I do abhor.

Oh, you might smile and you might feel
My story is a tickle,
But you imagine ev'ry meal
Made up of naught but pickle.

I cannot stand this little green
That sits upon my dish.
So ugly, salty, sour – obscene!
For something else I wish!

But though I long for bread or meat,
My wife's set in her ways,
And so these pickles I must eat
For all my lasting days.

When he had finished his sad little song, the merchant looked up to find a great crowd had gathered around him, and people were clapping along in amusement. Slightly cheered by this, he sang his ditty again, allowing the spectators to join in, until most of the market was humming the tune to themselves. In fact, he was so buoyed by sharing his sorry tale that the merchant returned to the market the next night, for he found singing about pickles far preferable to actually eating them.

If Kadija knew what was happening in the town – that her poor culinary skills had become a source of great mirth – she did not say, although the merchant thought he detected some sadness in her as he spurned her meals. Nevertheless, the next day he returned to the market for the third time, fully intending to sing his song once more. Only, when he arrived, someone already had the stage:

I must lament my recent find,
To all you market folk:
That a lady smart and kind
Is now a rotten joke.

Hearing the tune to his own song, slightly twisted with different words, caused the merchant to frown. The man singing was an older gentleman, a professor from the university, and he had the crowd enthralled:

Oh, smile and sing and laugh you might:
Although it makes me prickle,
But you imagine ev'ry night
Being mocked about a pickle.

So poor Kadija cannot cook!
Is that so very wrong?
She's better with a pen and book,
My student's mind is strong!

I used to wish, I used to pray,
I'd win this maid for life,
So to the man she chose, I'll say:
Be grateful for your wife.

As he sang this last line, the professor looked directly at the merchant, who felt a great rush of shame. For he realised that he had been cruel to publicly complain about his wife in the market, and felt very embarrassed that this other man had had to tell him so. Yet there was another emotion in the merchant's heart too, as he realised how this clever professor felt about Kadija: jealousy. The merchant did not want his neglect of her to cause a flirtation – or worse – between his wife and the professor. No, the merchant loved Kadija, despite her hopeless cooking, and knew now that to save his marriage he had to do something about their dinners.

'Thank you for showing me the error of my ways,' he told the professor, offering his hand.

The professor looked stern. 'If Kadija, my best student, had agreed to marry me, I would have gone hungry rather than upset her,' he said. 'I would have eaten the rubbish from the gutter, I would have *starved...*'

The merchant hung his head. 'I am very sorry for how I have acted,' he said.

'But it is not me that you need to apologise to, is it?' said the professor.

And the young merchant saw that he was right, and he knew that he had to find a way to atone for finding fault with his near-perfect wife. So he ran to the biggest restaurant in town and requested a great meal be prepared.

'Good sirs, give me your biggest lamb, one that has been stuffed and roasted for eight hours!' he cried. 'Give me four types of hummus! Give me five skewers of shish kebabs and a pyramid of kibbe! Give me baklava, give me kanafeh, and while you are about it, give me that delicious rice pudding, ruz balaib!'

The chefs were greatly surprised by this large order, but hurried to prepare and package all of the food into a great box for their enthusiastic customer. Then the merchant rushed back home to his wife, who was greatly surprised by the sudden appearance of both her husband and all this food.

'My dear Kadija!' said the merchant, falling to his knees. 'I have been a terrible fool! I have resented you for your lack of cooking ability, when I should have realised that everyone has their flaws. Rather than holding yours against you, I should have been celebrating all of your wonderful qualities: your kindness, your intelligence, your beauty. Will you forgive me?'

With tears in her eyes, Kadija nodded, and threw her arms gratefully around her husband's neck. Then, curiously, she asked, 'What is in the box?'

'A great feast, in honour of you, my love!' said the merchant. 'From now on, I will bring the food, and you will bring the conversation, does that sound fair?'

'That sounds fair,' she laughed.

'It seems this cooking problem is easily solved,' went on the merchant. 'We will eat in restaurants, we will order food to take back home, and certainly my dear mother can teach you – no, she can teach both of us – to cook. For how pleasant it will be to learn something like that together! Yes, I think our dinners will be very fine from now on, sweet Kadija!'

So together, the merchant and his wife sat down to the extraordinary meal that had been prepared for them, sharing the succulent meat and creamy hummus of the main course before moving on to the mouth-watering desserts. And while they smiled and talked and joked easily over all of the fine food, the merchant found that he was very glad indeed that he had finally chosen to marry – and almost as happy that he would never have to eat another pickle again.

The Mother-in-Law

Once upon a time there lived a widow who had three daughters. As their father had died many years before, the widow doted on her girls, and throughout their childhood she dedicated her whole self to their happiness and wellbeing. As they grew up, and became more independent, it pained this mother that they needed her less and less. Until, one fateful year, it just so happened that all three of her daughters got married, and each moved out of the family house within a few months of one another.

Naturally, their poor mother was devastated, especially as the timing was so unfortunate. She thought she could have suffered one girl moving out – maybe two at a stretch, providing they lived nearby – but to lose all three in such quick succession, it was more than the woman could bear. The night after her third daughter's wedding, her insides felt hollow, as though something was missing from her body. At first, she thought it might simply be hunger, but when she sat down to her first solitary meal, the miserable woman found she could not eat a single bite.

Of course, her daughters had not forgotten her, and a week later the oldest girl, who had married first, invited her mother round for dinner. As the girl opened the door of her new house, she thought her mother might have lost weight in the few days since her sister's wedding, but did not think any more of it, as she began to lay out a delicious meal of shish kebabs, hummus and tabbouleh.

Her mother, who had barely been able to eat much more than a few grains of plain rice over the past week, suddenly found that the hollowness inside her was gone, and the delicious smells wafting from the dishes on the table were making her feel starving. As her daughter chattered on about married life, the woman began to stuff the barbecued meat, chickpea dip and fattoush salad into her mouth as quickly as she could, hardly pausing to breathe between bites, and then helping herself to second and third portions. Her daughter noticed this rather uncouth behaviour, but instead of being alarmed, was rather pleased; apparently, her mother was eating just fine in her absence, and she clearly enjoyed her cooking, which the girl had been worried about.

By the time it was time to go, the woman was almost full to bursting, but she could not help but notice a whole string of spicy sausages hanging on a hook above the stove, presumably for the next day's meal. They were fat, red makanek sausages, a Levantine delicacy, and it did not matter that she was no longer hungry; the more she looked at those sausages, the more she wanted them – after all, what if she was cursed to only be able to eat her daughter's cooking from now on? Soon enough, the woman's mouth had begun to water at the idea of putting those tasty sausages into her pan at home, cooking them in oil, and gobbling down every single one.

She was too embarrassed to ask for the sausages outright, because she was afraid her daughter might take offence, but she was still determined to have them. So, after she had bade her daughter goodbye, she managed to slip the string of sausages from the hook before she left the house. Unfortunately, as she hurried outside, trying to cram the spicy sausages into her bag as she walked, she bumped into her new son-in-law, who was on his way back from work.

'Are those the makanek sausages that were hanging in my kitchen?' he asked, frowning down at her.

'Sausages?' said his mother-in-law. 'Why would I have your sausages? No, no, no, dear, this is my string of coral necklaces that I put together – look!'

And, as he watched, the woman draped the string of red sausages over her arms, and even threw one end over her neck with the flourish, as though it were very fancy indeed. Her son-in-law, who could see quite clearly that it was not a string of red coral necklaces but a string of uncooked sausages, did not know whether to be annoyed or amused by this charade. But in the end, he wanted to keep the peace with his mother-in-law, so he simply said, 'My mistake, of course it is a string of coral necklaces – and a lovely one too.'

Relieved and triumphant, the woman dashed back home. The next night, as she had promised herself, she cooked and ate the entire string of sausages, and for a little while she did not feel quite so lonely in her big, empty house. But after that, she could hardly bear to touch another bite of food, and so instead she counted down the days until she was invited to her second daughter's new house at the end of the week.

Like her sister before her, as this girl first saw her mother, she thought she looked rather thin, but was not particularly troubled by it as she began to lay out a delicious afternoon tea of kanafa, baklava, fruits and nuts.

As soon as she was faced with this food, the mother once more found the hollowness inside her was gone, and the beautifully arranged treats on the table were making her feel starving. As her second daughter chattered on about married life, the woman began to stuff the sweet cakes into her mouth as quickly as she could, almost choking in her eagerness to eat as much as possible, and then reaching across the table to help herself to second and third portions. Her daughter was a little taken aback by these questionable table manners, but she was as pleased as her sister had been, also deciding her mother's eagerness to eat was due to her own baking prowess.

By the time she was due to go, the woman was so full she felt a little sick, but she could not help but notice a whole plate of pistachio cookies sitting on the windowsill, presumably for the next day. It did not matter that she was no longer hungry; the more she looked at those cookies, the more she wanted them – after all, she was now certain the only food she could stomach was that made by her daughters. Soon enough, the woman's mouth had begun to water at the idea of laying out those cookies on a plate at home, pouring out a glass of fresh, cold milk, and then gobbling down every single one.

As before, she was too embarrassed to ask for the cookies outright, because she was afraid her daughter might take offence, but she was still determined to have them. So, when she had bade her daughter goodbye, she managed to slip the cookies from the plate. Unfortunately, as she hurried outside, she saw her second son-in-law coming back from his work and – panicked

— the woman stuffed the cookies into her mouth, but instead of swallowing them she pushed them in her cheeks, like a hamster.

The young man regarded his mother-in-law curiously, wondering why she suddenly looked so strange.

'Are you quite all right?' he asked.

The woman tried to reply, but her cheeks were stuffed so full she could not utter a single word. So instead, she beckoned for a piece of a paper, and wrote down the following words:

I have a medical condition that causes my cheeks to swell. Please forgive my appearance.

The son-in-law looked at this note, and knew at once she was talking nonsense, and there was nothing wrong with her. Furthermore, he had spoken to his brother-in-law a few days' earlier, who had told him the story of the sausages, and so he wondered whether something similar might be going on here. He said, 'It looks like a very serious medical condition to me. I think we should send for a doctor.'

But his mother-in-law shook her head, and wrote:

Please don't fetch the doctor, I'm terribly embarrassed. I'll go home and sleep it off, I'll be fine in the morning.

'Fair enough,' said the young man, hoping very much that his new wife didn't become like her mother in her old age. 'Well, I hope you feel better soon.'

Relieved and triumphant, the woman dashed back home, and immediately emptied what was left of the cookies from her cheeks. The next night, as she had promised herself, she ate them with a glass of cold, fresh milk, and for a little while she did not feel quite so lonely in her big, empty house. But once again, she could hardly bear to touch another bite of food for the rest of the week, and was very relieved to know that she would be going to the house of her third and youngest daughter in just a few days.

Meanwhile, the two sons-in-law who had caught the woman red-handed told their wives about the thefts of the cookies and the sausages, and the two girls were shocked to hear of their mother's behaviour. They in turn passed the tale onto their younger sister, the newest bride. She was the smartest of the three daughters, and while the others fretted, it was this youngest girl who hatched a plan to catch their mother in the act, and find out what on earth was going on.

Like her sisters before her, she laid out a delicious meal for her mother, this time of vine leaves stuffed so tightly with rice and spiced lamb they looked like fat fingers. And, for a third time, her guest devoured everything in sight, as if she hadn't eaten in a decade, abandoning her table manners completely. Of course, the girl had been forewarned of this, and did not bat an eyelid as her mother grabbed at every last scrap on the table. She did, however, make a point of sighing and saying, 'I am afraid this new house has a bit of a mouse problem, mother.'

'Oh?' said the woman, through a mouthful of rice.

'Yes, but don't worry, they haven't been at the food. You see, I keep it all up there, out of their reach.' The girl nodded up to a great copper dish, hung with chains, that was almost as wide as the table it was suspended over, alongside several pots and pans. 'It's not an ideal solution, but it'll have to do, until we can get a cat.'

'I see,' said her mother, who was far more interested in the food than what her daughter was saying.

Later though, when the meal was done, and the daughter was in the bathroom, the woman looked around for some edible keepsake to take from the house, as had become her custom. But she could not find a single morsel of food: all of the cupboards, the drawers, the tins and the jars were completely empty, and the pantry was locked. Then she remembered what her daughter had said, and realised that all of the house's food was stored unseen on the other side of that great copper dish hanging from the ceiling, next to the pots and pans.

She considered her predicament. The dish was suspended high above her head, and it would be a lot harder to get to than simply slipping a string of sausages from a hook, or taking a few cookies from a plate. But then she remembered how hungry she was during the days on which she didn't see her daughters, and though she was extremely full up, the mere thought of being alone made her feel all empty again.

So, after glancing through the door to make sure her daughter was not on her way back, the woman picked up a stool and put it on top of the table. Then she clambered onto both the table and the stool, and managed to stretch up towards the dish hanging from the ceiling. She grabbed onto the copper edge, pots and pans clattering loudly around it as she knocked against them, and then with a great heaving effort, she managed to pull herself up and over the side of the dish, and topple inside on top of all of the food it contained.

She had not been in there a minute when she heard the voice of her youngest daughter's husband: 'Ah,' he said, 'we seem to have caught a mother-in-law in our trap.'

The woman peeped out over the top of the dish. Standing in the kitchen and roused, no doubt, by the clinking of the pans, were all three of her daughters and all three of their husbands. They were staring up at her, their arms folded, their expressions stern. The woman realised she was caught, and burst into tears.

'I'm sorry!' she sobbed. 'I'm so sorry I stole your food! I've just been unable to eat any of my own cooking since you left the family home, and I've been so hungry! I think I must be very ill, and perhaps you should send for the doctor after all! But you must see, I miss cooking for you, and eating with you.'

'Oh mother, there's nothing wrong with you,' said the youngest daughter, pulling the chains and gently lowering the dish – and her mother – back to ground level. 'I see that you're lonely. You miss us, just as we miss you.'

The woman, who had expected her daughter to be very angry, cried even harder.

'But what shall I do?' she wailed. 'How shall I cope?'

'I think we should take it in turns to eat with you each night,' said the younger daughter.

'Providing you don't steal from us, of course,' added her husband, sharply.

'Yes,' agreed his wife. 'Those must be the terms. Perhaps, when you are feeling better, you might try eating on your own again, but only when you are ready. And we will all of us eat together every Sunday.'

The mother thought this a very agreeable plan indeed, as did the sisters. The three husbands had little choice but to agree, and generally thought it a tolerable solution, especially if it meant they wouldn't go without their cookies and their sausages. So every day, the poor widow had somebody to eat her evening meal with, and over time she found she didn't feel so hollow by herself after all, even though she never again stole as much as a crumb from any of her daughters.

Apples

Once upon a time, there were three sisters who each married within a year of one another. The eldest, who was the most beautiful, married a prince, and went to live on his grand estate. The middle sister, who was the cleverest, married a merchant, and went to live in his comfortable townhouse. And the youngest sister, who was the kindest, married a blacksmith, and went to live in a little room above his workshop.

Before the sisters left home, their mother, who was very wise, told each of them the same thing: 'In this town, there is an orchard where the trees bear the finest apples you have ever seen, smelled or tasted. My daughter, once you are married, eat at least one of these apples a day, for then you will bear children who are big and strong.'

The young women all assured their mother they would do this, and each of them set off for their new home.

After the eldest daughter was married, she sent a servant to the orchard to enquire about the fruit of which her mother had spoken. The servant reported back they were indeed the finest apples he had ever seen, smelled or tasted, but as such they were very expensive. However, the prince's wife now had plenty of money, and so she requested the servant bring her three shiny apples a day, which she ate throughout her pregnancy. When she later gave birth to a son, he was big and strong, and she named him Soumar.

After the middle daughter was married, she rode to the orchard on her husband's mule to enquire about the fruit of which her mother had spoken. There, she discovered the finest apples she had ever seen, smelled or tasted, but as such they were very expensive. However, the merchant's wife now had some money, and she returned to the orchard throughout her pregnancy so she had a supply of the shiny apples, enough to eat one a day. When she later gave birth to a son, he was of average height and build, and she named him Hayyan.

After the youngest daughter was married, she walked to the orchard to enquire about the fruit of which her mother had spoken, for she had neither a mule nor any servants. There, she discovered the finest apples she had ever seen, smelled or tasted, but as she was now a blacksmith's wife, she had very little money to spare. However, because she was kind, the gardener in the orchard took pity on her, and told her she could take the damaged and worm-eaten apples off his hands for a copper coin every couple of weeks. The young woman gratefully agreed to this deal, and after cutting away the bruises and holes, she ate merely a few slices of apple each day of her pregnancy. When she later gave birth to a son, he was very, very small, and she named him Touk.

They were a strange sight, this trio of cousins, and as they grew up, people would shake their heads in disbelief that the three boys could be related. Soumar was tall and strapping, although prone to arrogance, having been pampered by his wealthy parents and their servants. Hayyan worked hard to keep up with his older cousin, and although he was leaner and less tough, he had a keen, almost devious mind, and so Soumar appreciated his company.

But neither boy could stand their younger cousin, Touk. The dwarf was as kind as his mother and as diligent as his blacksmith father, but Soumar and Hayyan could not see past his strange, shrunken appearance, and were always ashamed to go out into the town with him.

Nevertheless, the cousins were encouraged by their mothers to spend time with one another, for those sisters had played happily together as children. Therefore the people of the town would often see Soumar and Hayyan running about and playing raucous games, while Touk trailed behind them, struggling to keep up on his little legs. When the older boys weren't ignoring their smaller relative, they would call him names and giggle at his deformity, and poor Touk put up with this bullying because he loved his cousins, and nobody else wanted to play with him.

As they grew older, the two bigger boys developed a taste for hunting on Soumar's father's estate, and they would saddle up magnificent Arabian horses, arm themselves with sabres and crossbows, and chase deer, boar and foxes through the woods until sunset. Touk, meanwhile, was forced to trot far behind them on the back of a goat, for all his uncle's horses were far too big for him, and as he was not strong enough to hold a sabre or crossbow, his only weapon was a child's catapult.

'How tired I am of that little wretch!' said Soumar to Hayyan, when the sun was setting on their day in the woods and they were waiting for Touk to catch up with them. 'How I wish he wouldn't follow us about everywhere! He looks so ridiculous on that goat. I am ashamed to call him my cousin.'

'As am I,' said Hayyan. 'Perhaps, then, it is time to make it clear we want nothing more to do with him.'

'What did you have in mind?' asked Soumar, for he knew his younger cousin was cleverer and more scheming than he.

'I suggest we do not wait for him,' replied Hayyan. 'If we gallop back to your father's house now, he will not be able to keep up with us, nor find his way out of the woods. Then, perhaps he will finally understand we do not want to spend any more time with him.'

Soumar thought this an excellent idea, and so together the older cousins kicked at their horses' flanks and galloped out of the woods.

When Touk finally reached the place where they had been supposed to meet, he could not understand why his cousins were not there, but trusting they would appear soon, he slid off his goat, sat down on a rock, and began to wait. He waited and waited until many hours had passed, the night had grown dark and cold, and it was only then Touk began to realise his cousins had abandoned him. He grew very frightened, for the woods were large and full of fearsome creatures, and he was little and only had his catapult to defend him. Crawling beside his goat for warmth and comfort, the dwarf began to cry bitterly.

'Little Man, why are you crying?' said a voice.

Touk sat bolt upright, fumbling with his catapult in case the newcomer meant him harm, and when he looked up he saw a dark-haired man in long traditional robes, his legs lost in wispy smoke.

'You may put the catapult down, I will not harm you,' said the stranger. 'Besides, little stones and rocks are no good against me, for I am a genie. But tell me, Little Man, why are you crying?'

'I am crying because my cousins are cruel to me,' sobbed Touk. 'They ignore me and mock me and call me names, just because I am small, and now they have abandoned me in these woods and I do not know the way home.'

'That is indeed unfortunate,' said the genie. 'But if I were to grant you a wish, you could have your revenge on them. Why, you could wish your cousins as small as you are – smaller, in fact.'

'Oh no!' cried Touk, alarmed. 'They wouldn't like that at all!'

'Why don't you wish them ugly, then?' suggested the genie. 'Or covered in boils? Or only able to cluck like chickens?'

'Oh no, no, no!' wailed Touk. 'They wouldn't like that at all! All I want is for them to stop being so cruel to me, and love me as I love them.'

The genie stroked his long beard thoughtfully. 'You are too kind, Little Man,' he said, rather disappointed, for genies are as mischievous as they are magical. 'But if you wish it, I will make it so.'

It just so happened, the following night, that the prince and his wife were hosting a great feast in the majlis of their house. Their son Soumar was, of course, invited to attend, as were his two cousins, although it was only Hayyan who turned up. Neither boy had seen Touk since they had left him in the woods the previous evening, although at first they were very pleased he had finally managed to grasp they didn't want his company.

'How nice it is, not to have that little imp following us about all the time,' said Soumar.

'Indeed!' agreed Hayyan. 'I feel as though I can hold my head up high in the streets, knowing he's not skulking about behind us.'

But as the evening wore on, and Touk did not appear, his cousins began to feel a little uneasy.

Once the feasting was done, a young musician arrived to entertain the guests as they lolled about on their cushions and drank sweet tea. He was a young man, with a dark beard, and in addition to his oud – a stringed instrument the shape of a pear, and similar in likeness to a lute – he carried with him a sack of belongings.

'I can sing a song about anything,' he boasted, to the assembled guests. 'Give me a topic, and I will sing about it.'

'Sing about me,' said Soumar, who was very arrogant. 'I deserve a song, because I am the heir to this estate.'

'I can do better than that,' said the musician, 'I can sing about you and your brother next to you.'

Soumar looked at Hayyan, who was sitting beside him.

'He is not my brother, he is my cousin,' the young man said.

'And there is a third cousin, my son,' said the blacksmith's wife, who was growing worried about her missing boy.

The musician strummed at his oud and said, 'Very well, I shall sing a song about three cousins. Does the third look like you?'

'Not at all,' said Soumar. 'He is a very little boy.'

'Speak plainly, cousin,' said Hayyan, 'he is a dwarf.'

There was laughter around the majlis, much to the annoyance of Touk's mother. The musician raised his eyebrows in amusement.

'A dwarf, did you say? How amusing! How droll! I should certainly like to sing a song about him. Does he look like a little beast?'

'No!' cried Soumar and Hayyan, who did not like this man coming into the majlis and insulting their relative. 'He is just little.'

'Well, if I am to sing about the dwarf, I should like to see him. Where is your little cousin?' asked the musician.

'We do not know,' admitted Soumar, feeling ashamed. 'We saw him in the woods yesterday, and he has been missing ever since.'

'How mysterious!' said the musician, his tone mocking. 'Well, I shall have to make up how ugly he is.'

'Don't you dare!' cried Hayyan, who was also feeling guilty about leaving Touk all alone in the woods.

'A different song, then,' said the musician.

'I don't think we want to hear any of your songs,' said Soumar.

But something curious was happening to the musician. Before their eyes, he was growing older, and his legs were turning to smoke. Then he took up his oud and started to sing:

Last night I drifted 'tween the trees,
Dark was the sky, cold was the breeze,
And there I met a little man,
Who'd been abandoned by his clan.
I watched him sob, I watched him shake,
I thought his heart would surely break,
And so I urged him to repay,
Those kin who'd galloped far away.
But that young dwarf, so poorly used,

He shook his head and he refused,
'They would not like that, not at all,'
This was his loyal mournful call.
And when I heard it I grew vexed,
(I thought those cousins should be hexed),
But as they weren't there to attack,
Instead I gathered up my sack.
I pushed the snivelling pup inside,
He could not flee – although he tried.
I went back home, took out my bowl…
And then I ate your cousin whole.

As the genie finished his song, he gave one last strum of the oud, and then grinned around at the horrified guests. Touk's mother fell into a dead faint, and Soumar and Hayyan both leapt to their feet, anguished.

'No, this can't be true!' they cried.

'I do not know why you are so upset,' said the genie. 'You wanted him gone, and now he is. What did you think would happen to a little man like him on his own in the woods?'

'It was just a joke!' said Soumar, his eyes filling with tears.

'We didn't mean anything by it!' added Hayyan.

'Perhaps I might have spared him, had he wished revenge on you,' said the genie, 'but he didn't even do that, so I had him for my dinner.'

Soumar and Hayyan began to cry.

'He might not have been tall or strong,' sobbed Soumar, 'but he was a better man than me.'

'And he might not have been clever,' sobbed Hayyan, 'but he was a better man than me too.'

The genie threw his sack towards them. 'I kept you his bones,' he said. 'Take them, and live with your guilt for the rest of your days.'

Still crying, Soumar and Hayyan took the sack, which was heavier than they had expected. Then, when they made to peer fearfully inside at their cousin's small bones, Touk himself tumbled out, very much alive and well.

'My cousins, forgive the genie and me for our trick, but I wanted you to stop being so cruel,' he said.

But his words were lost in the great commotion that had followed his sudden reappearance: everybody in the majlis had shouted in surprise and delight, Touk's mother had fainted again, and Soumar and Hayyan had both dropped to their knees to embrace their little cousin, now shedding tears of joy.

'Touk, you are alive!' cried Soumar. 'You are alive, and everything is well!'

'We will never be cruel to you again!' cried Hayyan. 'Not for as long as we live!'

And the two older boys stayed true to their word. Now, it was a common sight to see all three of them together in the streets, for Touk no longer lagged behind Soumar and Hayyan, and when they went hunting, the dwarf sat in a special saddle upon a fine Arabian horse, and wielded a custom-made crossbow. Although the three young men still looked different, they were now so often together, and so often laughing and joking with one another, nobody in the town had any doubts that Soumar, Hayyan and Touk were the closest of cousins.

The Vizier's Habit

Long ago, there lived a powerful sultan who was accompanied almost everywhere by his friend and advisor, the vizier. Now these two men were like chalk and cheese: the sultan was loud and boisterous, while the vizier was quiet and solemn. Yet perhaps because of their differences, the pair of them always rubbed along very well together.

Or rather, *almost* always, it should be said, because the vizier had a very irritating habit that never failed to set the sultan's teeth on edge: his instinctive response to everything – whether it be good news or bad, a funny joke or a sad story – was to sigh and say, 'Well, it is probably for the best.'

When the two men went hunting in the desert, and the sultan shot a gazelle, the vizier would sigh and say, 'Well, it is probably for the best.' But equally, he would say exactly the same thing if the sultan's arrow missed its target and the animal got away. When the two men ate a meal together, and the sultan was served the most delicious food, the vizier would sigh and say, 'Well, it is probably for the best.' But equally, he would say exactly the same thing if the sultan spat out his food in disgust. When the two men were discussing the progress of the kingdom's army, and they had won a great victory, the vizier would sigh and say, 'Well, it is probably for the best.' But equally, he would say exactly the same thing if the sultan's men had suffered a great defeat.

The sultan was always very annoyed by this stupid phrase that the vizier wheeled out for every occasion, but he just about tolerated it because the vizier was a good friend and advisor. Then, one day, the two men were out riding in the jungle when the sultan's horse tripped on some tree roots and the sultan was thrown to the ground. He landed awkwardly, and felt a blinding pain in his arm.

'Argh!' he cried, in agony. 'I think my arm is broken!'

The vizier, still atop his horse, peered down at him and sighed. 'Well, it is probably for the best,' he said.

The sultan's suffering was too great to respond to this, and he was rushed back to the palace for medical attention. But unfortunately, his injury was so serious that it became badly infected and, after a few weeks, the doctors were forced to cut off his arm to stop the infection spreading to the rest of his body.

The sultan was, of course, devastated by this turn of events, and sent for the vizier hoping that he would be cheering company. And although the vizier felt very sorry for his friend and king, somehow he could not help himself from sighing and muttering that same, exasperating phrase: 'Well, it is probably for the best.'

Upon hearing this, the sultan's mouth fell open with astonishment, aghast that the man could say such a thing even now.

'No, it is *not* for the best!' he exploded at the vizier. 'I have lost my arm, you fool, you idiot, you complete dunderhead! I should have you executed for your insolence!'

The vizier fell upon his knees, very much afraid. 'Please, Your Majesty, forgive me. It is but a saying—'

'Well, I never want to hear it again!' shouted the sultan. 'You are dismissed – get out, leave my sight before I change my mind about chopping off your head.'

And the vizier, anxious to leave with his head still attached to his shoulders, hurried away.

A few months passed and the sultan slowly recovered, though he was still deeply upset about the loss of his arm. Also, though he was too proud and too angry to invite him back to the palace, the sultan missed his friend and advisor, the vizier – though not, of course, his silly phrase.

Once he was well enough, the sultan decided to go hunting to take his mind off his misery and loneliness. He and a manservant rode deep into the jungle, hoping to find some exotic creature to shoot, and they were searching for so long that they accidentally strayed over the boundary of the kingdom and into cannibal territory. Suddenly, they were set upon by a tribe of fearsome man-eaters, who tied up the sultan and his manservant and carried them back to their camp.

'This one looks like a tasty meal,' the cannibals said, pinching and sniffing at the manservant. 'Put him in the pot, cook him, and let us eat him all up!'

And, to the sultan's great horror, that is exactly what they did.

'Oh dear!' the sultan said to himself, as the cannibals slept off their meal. 'What shall I do? How will I get out of this terrible situation? Oh, the fear! The shame! Even if I am ready to face death – which I am not – being eaten by cannibals is a very dishonourable end for a sultan. My legacy will be ruined!'

He worried about this for the whole of the night until, come the dawn, the cannibals awoke and came to inspect their next victim.

'This one looks like a tasty meal,' they said, pinching and sniffing at the sultan. 'Put him in the pot, cook him, and – urgh! What is this?'

For they had finally noticed the stub at the sultan's shoulder where his arm had once been, and the sight of it seemed to disgust them.

'He is mutilated! He is misshapen! He is deformed!' the cannibals cried. 'Yuck, we cannot eat him now – he would be an imperfect meal! Urgh!'

And, to the sultan's great surprise and relief, they untied him and let him go free.

For half a day he stumbled back through the jungle, thanking God for his release and trying to find his way back to the palace. Then, when he had finally returned home, been checked over by doctors, and had a hearty vegetarian meal (the thought of meat made him feel a little queasy after his adventure), the sultan summoned his old vizier.

The man arrived promptly and listened in alarm and amazement at the extraordinary story of what had happened to the sultan and his poor manservant. He also listened with his hand clamped over his mouth, so as not to risk execution by uttering that hated phrase. The sultan noticed this and smiled.

'My friend, remove your hand and say what you like. For that is why I asked you here today: to tell you that you were right. When my arm was amputated, you infuriated me by saying, "Well, it is probably for the best." But it turns out that, if I had been whole when those cannibals had captured me, they would certainly have cooked and eaten me by now. So my injury *was* for the best, after all. Perhaps you can forgive me my temper, especially as I have had such a terrible time?'

The vizier lowered his hands from his mouth. 'Of course, I am just glad you are alive and safe,' he said. 'Goodness me – captured by cannibals!' Then, seemingly without thinking, he sighed and added, 'Well, it is probably for the best.'

The sultan shook his head, laughing. 'I'm not sure my late manservant would agree with you there – I shall have to offer my condolences and perhaps some gold to his family. But in terms of our friendship, and the fact we are now reconciled, yes – I suppose my capture by cannibals probably was for the best after all!'

Sons and Seasons

There was once a farmer who owned a great deal of land and, as he grew older, he began to worry about who could take it on after him. The farmer had four sons, but although they were his natural successors, he worried that they did not understand the responsibility of caring for fields of crops, orchards of fruit and grazing animals. Since his poor wife had died, the farmer had indulged his boys, letting them play all day long rather than having them do chores around the land, and as such they seemed to have no notion of the family business. This was all well and good while the farmer was still fit and healthy, but as the boys grew up and he grew into middle age, he knew that something had to change.

So one day, when all the work of the harvest was finally done for the year, the farmer called all four of his sons into his study.

'My boys,' he said, 'you are almost men now, and while I am proud of all that you have become, I believe that you still have a lot to learn about life. So what I want you to do is this: go out into the world on your own and explore, and when you are done, come back and tell me what you have learned.'

The four boys stared at him in confusion.

'But where shall we go?' asked the oldest son.

The farmer opened up his arms. 'Wherever you like,' he said.

'But how shall we live?' asked the second son.

The farmer held out four leather pouches. 'With this gold from the recent harvest,' he said.

'But how shall we know when we have finished exploring?' asked the third son.

The farmer smiled. 'You will know,' he said.

They all looked to the youngest brother, who had not yet spoken.

'Son,' the farmer asked his smallest boy, 'do you have anything to ask?'

But the youngest, who was perhaps the wisest of them, shook his head. 'No, father, I understand what I am to do.'

So off they went, the four young men, leaving the comfort of their home far behind and heading out into the world. The farmer waved them off cheerfully as he and his workers watched them march away in their separate directions – north, east, south and west – although in his heart he feared that the boys were ill-prepared for what lay beyond the boundaries of the farm.

A few months passed, during which the weather turned cold and the farmer tried to get used to being in his empty house alone, without the boisterous bustle of his four children. Then, one bleak, snowy day, there was a knock at the door and he knew that one of his boys had returned.

When the farmer opened the door, it was his oldest son, a young man of twenty, who tripped through and headed straight towards the warmth of the fire.

'Father, I've come home!' he said, warming his hands in front of the flames.

'Yes, I see that,' said the farmer. 'And what did you learn on your travels, my son?'

'Oh, plenty,' said the boy with a great shudder. 'Father, I took the north road, and the further I went, the worse everything seemed. The sky was grey, the wind was bitter and the rain and sleet were unrelenting. The ground beneath my feet was hard and barren, while the trees above my head were so bare they looked like skeletons. Father, it was so miserable – if that is what the world is like beyond our farm, I do not think I wish to leave our land again. I now truly value my home, and that is what you were trying to teach us, was it not?'

The farmer hesitated. 'Perhaps, my boy, perhaps not. But, I am glad you are safely home. Now, go and fetch some oats from the cellar and we will make some warming porridge together.'

Then a few more months passed, during which the weather turned a little warmer, and the farmer became used to having just one son in the almost-empty house. Then, one crisp but sunny day, there was a knock at the door and he knew that another of his boys had returned.

When the farmer opened the door, it was his second oldest son, a young man of eighteen, who tumbled through and headed straight to the kitchen table.

'Father, I've come home!' he said, sitting down in his favourite chair.

'Yes, I see that,' said the farmer. 'And what did you learn on your travels, my son?'

'Oh, plenty,' said the boy with a slight smile. 'Father, I took the east road, and the further I went, the worse everything seemed – at first.'

The farmer's son went on to describe the early part of his travels in a similar manner to his older brother, explaining that everything had been very cold and grey.

'It made me so unhappy that I almost came home,' he confessed, 'but I did not think that I was done yet, so on I went. And eventually, the sky began to turn a little bluer, the wind began to lessen, and the rain felt fresh. The ground beneath my feet started to come alive with shoots and buds, while the trees above my head were bursting into pink and white blossoms. Father, it was so hopeful. I now truly value the way the land can start to renew itself, and I think that is what you were trying to teach us, was it not?'

Once more, the farmer hesitated. 'Perhaps, my boy, perhaps not. But, I am glad you are safely home. Now, go and pick some vegetables from the patches outside and we will make a fresh salad together.'

Then yet more months passed, during which the weather turned scorching hot, and the farmer became used to having two of his sons back in the house. Then, one dry, hot day, there was a knock at the door and he knew that another one of his boys had returned.

When the farmer opened the door, it was his third son, a young man of sixteen, who stood fanning himself on the threshold.

'Father, I've come home!' he said, drifting into the cool of the house.

'Yes, I see that,' said the farmer. 'And what did you learn on your travels, my son?'

'Oh, plenty,' said the boy, wiping a hand over his perspiring brow. 'Father, I took the south road, and the further I went, the worse everything seemed – at first.'

The farmer's third son then went on to describe the early part of his travels in a similar manner to both of his older brothers, explaining that everything had been very cold and grey, before he had witnessed a regeneration in the land.

'But I did not think that I was done yet, so on I went,' he said. 'And eventually, there was not a cloud in the sky, not a breath of wind, nor any sign of rain. The ground beneath my feet was lush and green, while the trees above my head were full of leaves and fruit. Father, it was like paradise, I felt lazy and relaxed and wanted to stay there forever. I now truly value the abundance of the land, and I think that is what you were trying to teach us, was it not?'

For the third time, the farmer hesitated. 'Perhaps, my boy, perhaps not. But, I am glad you are safely home. Now, go and pick some fruit from the orchard and we will make a sweet pie together.'

A few months after this, almost a year had passed since the farmer had sent his four sons out into the world, and now that three of them had returned the house almost felt full again. Yet he felt the absence of his other son keenly, and he was anxious to know what the youngest of his boys had discovered.

The weather turned a little colder, the harvest began, and then one golden day there was a knock at the door and the farmer knew that the last of his boys had returned.

When the farmer opened the door, it was, of course, his fourteen-year-old son who stood tall and calm beyond the doorway.

'Father, I've come home,' he said, and moved to fondly embrace the farmer.

'Yes, I see that,' said the farmer, a slight tear in each eye. 'And what did you learn on your travels, my son?'

'Oh, plenty,' said the boy, looking steadily out of the window at the land beyond the farm. 'Father, I took the west road, and the further I went, the worse everything seemed – at first.'

The farmer's youngest son then went on to describe the early part of his travels in a similar manner to all of his older brothers, explaining that everything had been very cold and grey, before he had witnessed a regeneration and then great abundance in the land.

'But I did not think that I was done yet, so on I went,' he said. 'And eventually, clouds began to gather in the sky, the wind returned and rain began to splash down upon my face. The ground beneath my feet and the trees above my head became covered in red and gold leaves. Father, not only did I find it beautiful to look at, I realised something : this was how the land had looked when I left the farm, all that time ago. I have now seen nature in all of its guises, and I think that is what you were trying to teach us, was it not?'

This time, the farmer did not hesitate. Instead, he gathered all four of his sons around the kitchen table and said, 'Now you have all returned, let us discuss what you learned.'

'I have learned that the land can be cold and cruel, and so we should appreciate our home,' said the first son.

'I have learned that the coldness passes and the land rejuvenates itself in new growth,' said the second son.

'I have learned that this new growth leads to a period of great warmth and abundance,' said the third son.

The youngest son looked thoughtful. 'I saw all of this on my travels, but witnessed something else too: after the hottest, most fruitful time, there is another change, another transition, so the cycle of the land can begin all over again.'

The farmer leaned back in his chair, beaming around at them with pride. 'You have all done very well, my sons,' he said. 'Now I think you truly understand each of the seasons – Winter, Spring, Summer and Autumn. But what is perhaps more important still is what you discovered,' he continued, looking at his youngest boy, 'for these seasons move in a cycle, round and round, each of them essential to the growing of crops and the rearing of animals. To see this is to start understanding how to care for the land – how to be a farmer – which I hope is something you will all wish to do one day.'

'Not one day, now!' cried all the boys.

And the farmer smiled, for he saw that his plan had worked, and in sending them out into the world to learn about the seasons his sons had gained an appreciation for the land and the role of a farmer.

'Well, we will have to wait until Spring to sow the seeds,' their father told them, 'but there are plenty of other chores to be done in the fields, orchards and pens. Come on!'

So, without wasting another minute, he led his four sons outside, and set to teaching them how to be successful farmers themselves.

The Foolish Wife

There was once a man named Hamza, who one night sat down at his table and counted out a large amount of gold coins. He then put the coins into a little leather pouch and handed it to his wife.

'My dear,' Hamza said, 'this pouch contains most of our savings. Would you please lock it away in the chest under our bed? I am saving it for Ramadan, so you must only fetch the pouch when Ramadan comes around.'

The Ramadan Hamza spoke of is the ninth month in the Islamic calendar, when everyone must fast between dawn and sunset, as well as offering extra prayers to God. However, before the sun rises and after it sets, all the people come together to eat, and there are many splendid feasts throughout the land. It was for these happy occasions that Hamza wished to save, in order that his friends and family might gather to eat and pray during this holy time.

His wife did as she was asked, and Hamza thought no more about it, until the month of Ramadan was almost upon them, and he requested that she fetch the coins from the chest under their bed.

'It is almost time for the fasting and the feasting to begin,' he told her, 'so I would like you to fetch me the pouch of coins, in order that we may feed all of our friends and family.'

At his words, Hamza's wife looked confused. 'But the coins are gone,' she said. 'I gave them to Mr Ramadan, when he came round, just as you asked me.'

Hamza stared at her in horror. 'You mean, you gave our coins for the holy time to a stranger called Mr Ramadan, who happened to call at the door? Oh God, you have cursed me with the most foolish wife in the world!'

And he was so angry that he pulled at his hair, gnashed his teeth together, and left the house with a slam of the door.

'I must find another wife,' Hamza told himself, as he strode along the dusty street. 'I cannot live with my own any longer, she is far too foolish. No, I must find a new wife, a clever one.'

Hamza was so agitated that he had walked all the way out of his village and was now well on his way to the next. As it came into view, he smiled.

'Ah, here in this neighbouring village, I will find a clever wife,' he said, and walked towards it.

The day was very hot, and Hamza was tired from the walk, so he searched for some shade, finally finding it under some trees by the stream. Yet he was not alone. Also sheltering under the trees were two women who looked to be sisters, one of whom was holding a baby of around six months.

Hamza could not help but notice that both of the women were extremely beautiful and although the one holding the baby obviously had a husband, he wondered whether her sister might be unmarried, and therefore free to be his new wife. Yet as he approached, intending to introduce himself, Hamza noticed something particularly strange: both of the women were crying.

'Excuse me?' he said, concerned. 'Is everything all right? I cannot help but notice that you seem very upset.'

Indeed, the two women were wailing and clutching at one another as though their hearts might break.

'It is my child,' sobbed the woman with the baby, 'he is going to die.'

Hamza gasped. 'How terrible!' he said. 'Is he sick? Has he an illness?'

The mother, who was too upset to say any more, merely shook her head.

'He is not sick,' said the sister, the one to whom Hamza hoped to propose. 'He does not have an illness.'

Hamza looked at the baby, who seemed to be a perfectly strong and healthy-looking child. 'Then how do you know he is going to die?' he asked, perplexed.

'Because it is inevitable,' continued the child's aunt. 'We have talked and talked on the matter, and we believe that what will happen is he will grow up to be twelve years old, climb up this tree under which we sit, then he will fall into this river and drown.' She burst into a fresh wave of tears. 'It is such a tragedy!'

Hamza stared at them both, and at the baby gurgling in their arms. 'That is absurd,' he said, 'you cannot plan this stupidity for twelve years. You cannot worry about life like that and not live it. You are both very foolish indeed.'

Even more foolish, he thought, then his own foolish wife, and without another word he left the crying women under the tree.

Hamza decided to walk to the next village in his quest to find a clever wife. When he arrived there, dusty and hot from the road, he was very thirsty, so decided to find a coffee house where he could buy a drink. He was pleased to see that, in the coffee house, there were four very beautiful women, one of whom Hamza thought could be a clever wife to him.

However, as he sat down with his coffee, Hamza saw that the four women were all pulling at their hair and crying out to one another as though a great drama were unfolding in their lives.

'Excuse me?' said Hamza, concerned. 'Is everything all right? I cannot help but notice that you seem very upset.'

One of the women pushed a little boy of around eight years old towards Hamza and said with a moan, 'It is my son! His hand has become stuck in this pot and now we must fetch a doctor to cut off his arm. My poor boy will go through life with only one arm!'

The boy, who had heard all of this and was crying with fright, did indeed have his arm stuck in a pot. Hamza knelt down beside him.

'Hello there, young man,' he said to the boy. 'How did your hand become stuck in that pot?'

The boy stopped his snivelling and looked at Hamza. 'I was reaching inside for sweets,' he said, 'I wanted them so badly, but now my hand won't come out.'

His mother gave a great scream of grief. 'And now it has cost him his arm!'

Hamza ignored her and continued to talk to the little boy. 'I think,' he began thoughtfully, 'that if your hand is small enough to go in there, it's small enough to come out. Do you still have the sweets in your hand?'

The boy nodded.

'Why don't you let them go, so your hand is no longer a fist.'

The boy did so and was then easily able to withdraw his hand from the pot.

'There,' said Hamza, picking up the pot from the ground, 'and if you hold out your hands, I can tip the sweets into your palms.'

The boy's mother, her friends, and everyone at the coffee shop were extremely grateful for Hamza's help, especially as the doctor no longer needed to cut off the child's arm. In fact they were so pleased, they asked him if there was anything they could do for him in return. Hamza considered asking for one of the beautiful women to be his new wife, but he had already decided that all the people in the coffee shop were incredibly foolish, and so he decided to try his luck at the next village instead.

As he walked, Hamza noticed that the early evening sky was less clear than it had been a few hours earlier, and clouds were gathering around the horizon. Nevertheless, he continued on, and when he reached the next village he was very tired from all his walking, so he searched for somewhere to sit down.

However, everyone else in the village seemed to be on their feet, running about and waving their hands in the air, screaming at the top of their lungs. Hamza approached the nearest person, an old man who was shaking from head to foot.

'Excuse me?' said Hamza, concerned. 'Is everything all right? I cannot help but notice that you seem very upset.'

The man fell to his knees, pointing at the sky. 'Look, look!' he cried. 'The sun is turning red, the clouds are turning black, the wind is howling – there is going to be another war!'

'A war?' said Hamza. 'Why, there hasn't been a war for fifty years.'

'That is precisely why one is about to start!' cried a younger man, running past.

'Look at the sky, look at the sky!' shouted a girl. 'It's a sign that war is coming!'

Hamza realised he could do nothing for these people, and that everyone in the village must be very foolish in order to predict wars by bad weather. Without another word, he turned on his heel and left.

It was a long walk back to Hamza's village, but Hamza didn't mind, for it gave him time to think. He had visited three villages that day, and encountered a great number of people far more foolish than his wife. In fact, now he came to think about it, in comparison to the wailing mothers and the villagers predicting battles that would never come, she seemed positively wise. He did love her very much, despite her mistake, so he decided to make peace with her as soon as he returned home.

Yet when Hamza walked through his front door, a surprise was waiting for him. Many of his family and friends were gathered around his kitchen table, drawing up a list.

'What is going on, my dear?' he asked, kissing his wife on the cheek.

'I told everyone of my foolish mistake with Mr Ramadan,' she explained, 'and how we now have no funds for a feast, and everyone agreed they would make a little of the meal themselves, and we will bring it all together to make the most wonderful celebration of Ramadan.'

And so Hamza realised that, while his wife might have been a little foolish, she was also sweet and thoughtful and benevolent, not to mention beloved amongst their family and friends, and he knew that that was far more important.

The Coin Collector

Once upon a time, a father, mother and their son lived on a small farm far away from the nearest city. They had a cow for milk, hens for eggs, and a garden for vegetables, so although they were not rich, they had enough to live comfortably, and a little money to buy a loaf of bread and a few essentials each week.

When the son reached the age of sixteen, the father decided it was time for him to find work. The boy had been mollycoddled by his mother all his life, and his father was worried that if this treatment continued he would never learn to stand on his own two feet. So he took his son aside, and said, 'It is time for you to leave home and learn independence. You must go to the city and find work. You may come back to us, but only when you have made a little money.'

The boy was very disheartened to hear that he would have to leave the comfort of the farm, although he was not as grieved as his mother, whose heart ached at the thought of being parted from her only child. When her husband was out in the fields, she slipped a coin into her son's hand and said, 'Here, take this gold coin. Now you can come back to us after a day, because you can tell your father you earned that money in the city.'

The boy thought this was an excellent idea, and did as she suggested: he set out in the direction of the city, waving goodbye to his mother and father, and then when the little house was out of sight he went to snooze in a nearby field. A day later, he returned to the farm with his mother's coin warm in his palm.

'Father, I have made a little money,' he said, showing his elder the gold coin.

The farmer took one look at the coin, before seizing it from his son's hand and throwing it out of the window.

'You come back to us with just one gold coin?' he said. 'Do you think this farm can run on just that? It is not enough! You must work harder! Go back to the city and earn more!'

Again, the boy was miserable at the idea of leaving his easy life, and his mother shuddered at the thought of saying goodbye to him again.

'Here, take these three gold coins,' she said, slipping the money into the boy's hand when her husband was outside. 'Now you can come back to us after a few days, because you can tell Father you earned that money in the city by working harder.'

Once more, the boy thought this a wonderful idea and did as she suggested: he set out in the direction of the city, waving goodbye to his mother and father, and then when the little house was out of sight he went to amble through the nearby villages. He knew it would look suspicious if he returned in just a day with three gold coins, so he tried to kill time for three days in the surrounding area. It soon became very boring, wandering around aimlessly, and the boy grew so restless he considered actually travelling into the city to do as his father wished. But the prospect of that big, busy place was too intimidating, so instead he walked and he snoozed, and then returned to his family's farm after three days.

'Father, I have made more money,' he said, showing his elder the three gold coins.

For a second time, the farmer took the coins and threw them out of the window.

'You come back to us with just three gold coins?' he cried. 'Do you think this farm can run on only that? And do you think you can assure your future that way? It is not enough! You must work harder! Go back to the city and earn more!'

Now, the boy was unhappier than ever, but he knew his mother would help him, so he went to her while his father was milking the cow and said, 'Mother, give me more money, and then I will stay away for a week. Surely he will be satisfied with five gold coins.'

But the woman began to cry. 'Son, I do not have five gold coins!' she wept. 'I do not even have one! I have already given you everything we have! I think you will have to go into the city and do what he asks.'

With a heavy heart, the boy set off for a third time, waving goodbye to his mother and father, and this time he continued on along the road to the city. He stayed away for a long time; longer than a week, longer than even a month, and when he finally returned to the farmhouse he looked thinner, but also older, and prouder too.

'Well?' said his father. 'Did you make any money?'

The boy emptied his purse onto the table: out tumbled just two silver and four copper coins. His mother began to cry.

'Is that all?' said his father.

'That is all I have left,' said the boy. 'I went to the city, as you told me to, and I got a job as an apprentice in a tannery. It was hard work, and the little pay I received went on food, and rent, and clothes and tools for my new trade. But it was good, father. I am learning a skill, and I have been promised more pay and a better position in the near future, so then I will give you more money.'

He prepared for his father to throw the measly money he had earned out of the window, but instead his elder picked up each coin in turn and kissed it.

'You are happy?' asked the son.

'This is worth a hundred times more than the gold you gave me before, because you earned it yourself. I had guessed that you didn't work, because you came back too quickly. Finally, I have a son who works hard, who is independent, and who has a future.'

With tears in his eyes, he embraced his boy, and then the little family sat down to a delicious home-cooked meal before, gladly, the son returned to his new home in the city.

Ahmed and the Mountain

There once lived a boy named Ahmed, who was so shy he didn't like playing with the other children. He found their voices too loud and their games too rough, and he preferred to go wandering off into the countryside on his own and write about what he found there in his journal.

Although Ahmed was perfectly happy to spend his childhood in this manner, his mother began to worry that he was lonely, so she bought him a kid goat to keep him company. The kid goat was small and snowy white, and so young it needed feeding from a bottle. Just as his mother had hoped, Ahmed was delighted with his new pet, and could often be seen leading it on long walks in the mountains by a piece of rope.

As Ahmed grew older, he began to gain a reputation as a very fine poet. His writings about nature were particularly well-received, and publications began to request that Ahmed pen poetry for them. He even had to overcome a little of his shyness, for there was great demand to hear him read his work aloud in cafes and on street corners. Even the sultan was an appreciator of his work, and one day he summoned Ahmed all the way to the palace to discuss a new opportunity.

'Young man, how much do you earn a week from this poetry?' he asked.

'A few silver coins, at most,' the writer replied. 'But that is all I need to keep my mother, my goat and me living comfortably.'

'How comfortable will you be if I paid you ten gold coins a day?' asked the sultan.

Ahmed stared at him in surprise. 'To write poetry?' he asked.

'I very much hope you will continue writing poetry in your spare time,' said the ruler. 'But what I would like you to do for me is take the position of Minister of Rural Affairs.'

Ahmed still did not understand. 'But I am a writer, your majesty. I know nothing of politics.'

'All the better, Ahmed,' replied the sultan. 'I have had several ministers of rural affairs over the past few years, and not one of them has understood the very thing they are supposed to make decisions about: the land. But I have read your poetry, and I know you appreciate how important it is to keep our rivers clean, our forests well-managed, and our fields harvested at the right time and in the right way. So that is why I would like you to become Minister of Rural Affairs.'

Ahmed did not need very long to think about this: ten gold coins a day was a huge amount of money, and if he could continue to write poetry in his spare time, all the better. So he accepted the sultan's kind offer, and he moved to the capital, where he began his new job.

For a year or so, Ahmed was content. He encouraged farmers to grow a bigger variety of crops, he approved the planting of many more orchards, and he instructed canals to be built to improve the transportation of food across the land. In this way, he quickly proved himself a knowledgeable and popular leader, and the countryside flourished under his care. He was also pleased to know that his mother, to whom he sent back most of his gold, was living a very easy life back in his home town.

The only blight on his happiness occurred when his mother wrote to him to tell him his beloved goat had died of old age. Under Ahmed and his mother's care, the animal had lived to fifteen, which was a long time for a goat, but this did not ease Ahmed's heartache over the news. After receiving his mother's letter, he wept all night over the loss of his oldest friend, and wished he had been in his home town for the goat's final days.

Ahmed was still grieving for the loss of his goat a few days later, when he was taking a tour of the countryside with a local farmer. Together, they walked up to a meadow on the land's tallest mountain, and Ahmed gave a cry of horror as he saw, under one of the olive trees, the body of a dead goat. It was, of course, not his beloved pet, but a younger animal with black patches. But still, the sight was very upsetting to him, especially so soon after his own goat's demise.

'What happened here?' he demanded of the farmer. 'How did this goat die?'

'I think it was trying to jump up into the tree,' explained the other man. 'I imagine it was trying to eat the leaves and fruit on the high branches, but it fell and broke its neck.'

'But why did it have to jump?' demanded Ahmed. 'Why did it not clamber up by the lower branches?'

The farmer pointed out a cover wrapped around the tree trunk and lower branches.

'These covers protect the trees from being eaten by goats and other animals,' he said.

But Ahmed was still greatly upset about the dead goat and flew into a temper about the tree covers.

'No, no, no!' he cried. 'As Minister of Rural Affairs, I forbid the use of these tree covers! I declare that goats may roam freely and eat whatever they like!'

The farmer tried to protest, but Ahmed was already storming down the mountainside to draft this legislation. Before long, just as he had promised, Ahmed had passed a law that goats must be allowed to roam freely and eat whatever they liked, and as a result all of the tree covers were torn down.

Not long after Ahmed's law came to pass, people across the land started to groan and grumble about the behaviour of the goats. Now they were free to roam freely and eat whatever they liked, the animals wandered into people's houses and gobbled the dinners off their plates, and they tramped through fields and tore up crops from the ground with their teeth. Humans grew hungry, whole farms were ruined, and the goat population grew and grew, because the creatures were so content and well-fed that many more goat kids were being born.

After receiving a barrage of complaints, the sultan gently suggested to Ahmed he might have made a rare mistake, in passing this law to protect the rights of goats. But Ahmed refused to listen, and he refused to back down; it filled him with great joy to watch all of the happy goats now gambolling around the land, especially as he was still mourning the loss of his dear pet.

Then a strange thing occurred. One night, there was a huge storm; rain lashed down on the land, and wind howled through the towns, farms and forests, rattling every house and shaking every tree in its path. When the people of the capital awoke the next day, tired and shivering after a cold night of fractured sleep, they looked out of their windows to discover that their tallest mountain had disappeared. They rubbed at their eyes, unable to believe what they were seeing: the day before it had been right there, on the horizon, stretching majestically into the clouds; now, it was completely gone.

As the morning wore on, the people began to panic. Where had the mountain gone? Had someone taken it? Was this an act of God? Were they being punished for their sins? As hysteria began to spread, the sultan summoned Ahmed to the palace.

'As Minister of Rural Affairs, I believe this is your responsibility,' he said. 'That mountain has been there since the days of Jesus, since the days of Moses and Mohammad, and now it has gone. Find out what has happened, Ahmed: mountains should not just disappear overnight.'

Ahmed promised he would do what he could, and he employed three experts to go to the dusty spot where the mountain had once been and investigate what had happened. They duly set off, but when they returned a few days later to report back, the three men looked at their feet and grew as shy as Ahmed had been as a child.

'Well,' said the minister, 'spit it out: what happened to the mountain?'

'It blew away,' said the first expert, stepping forward.

Ahmed laughed. 'What are you talking about?' he asked. 'How can a mountain blow away?'

The second expert stepped forward. 'We know from our studies that the earth in the mountainside was very fine, like chalk or sand. When the storm came, the wind blew up all of this soil, and swept it out towards the desert. That is what happened to our mountain; that is why it disappeared.'

'But that is ridiculous!' said Ahmed. 'That mountain has been there for thousands of years, why would it suddenly be swept away by the wind now?'

The three experts looked at one another, their expressions uncomfortable. Then the third man stepped forward.

'Until recently, the chalky soil was packed down tightly by a complex system of tree roots,' he said. 'When the tree roots went, the earth had nothing to hold it together, and so the wind dispersed it.'

'And where did the tree roots go?' demanded Ahmed. 'You can't tell me those blew away as well?'

'No, Sir,' said the third expert. 'The tree roots – and most of the trees themselves, in fact – were all eaten by goats.'

Ahmed's mouth fell open with shock and horror as he understood his part in the mountain's mysterious disappearance. He went at once to the palace and threw himself on the mercy of the sultan.

'Your Majesty, it is all my fault! The mountain blew away because all the goats ate the tree roots that were holding together the soil!' he cried.

The sultan was not best pleased to hear this. 'I should have you executed for stupidity,' he told Ahmed. 'You have destroyed a national landmark. But I see I am partly to blame for hiring someone so inexperienced for the role of Minister of Rural Affairs, so instead you are dismissed. Get out of my palace, Ahmed, and never come to the capital again.'

Miserably, Ahmed obeyed this order and returned to his hometown. For many days, weeks and months, he tried to think of a way to put right what he had done, but it was no good: the soil had been scattered over the desert outside of the country, and even if it could be collected up, piled together, and planted with trees, Ahmed knew enough to understand men could not make mountains. After a while, he was forced to accept there was little he could do to make amends, and that his career in politics was over, so he moved back in with his mother. He wrote a little poetry from time to time, but mostly they lived off the gold she had saved during the time he had been a minister, which was enough for them to keep comfortably, and for Ahmed to buy a new kid goat.

As for the sultan, after he had reversed Ahmed's law about allowing goats to roam freely and eat whatever they liked, he looked for a new minister. As Ahmed had been so disastrous in the job, the Sultan decided to abandon his idea of hiring someone with a love of the land, and instead chose an experienced man who demonstrated no affection for the great outdoors. Furthermore, before an agreement was reached, the sultan double-checked his new minister was wholly indifferent to goats.

THE FLEA MARKET

Once upon a time there were two brothers called Kareem and Hamza. They were seven and eight years old respectively, and because they were so close in age, many people thought they must be twins. Their father was a very clever scholar, but unfortunately his profession did not pay very much, so the family were poor and Kareem and Hamza were often obliged to go to school in stitched-up second-hand clothes.

School was the one thing the two brothers hated above all else. They liked to learn, and because they were only a year apart they were in the same class, and permitted to sit next to one another. But their teacher was the nastiest man the boys had ever encountered. He was tall, thin and bald, and his black-eyed gaze was always darting around the class on the hunt for troublemakers. If a child so much looked at him in a way he did not like, the teacher would summon that boy to the front of the class, whip out his silver cane, and thrash the unfortunate youngster across the back of the legs until he cried.

One day, when the boys were having their lunchbreak, Kareem tugged at his older brother's sleeve.

'Hamza, look at my shoes. They are completely worn through, and my feet are wet,' he said.

Hamza looked down at his brother's shoes. They were indeed falling apart: the sole had come loose and Kareem's toes were sticking out the front. As there had been a lot of rain over the past few days, Hamza thought his little brother's feet much be soaked through.

'Those shoes are completely useless. We must buy you a new pair,' he said.

'But mother and father don't have any money!' said Kareem.

Hamza thought about this, and then said, 'Why don't we visit the flea market in town. We have a few copper coins between us, from our pocket money. I am sure there must be a pair of old shoes there that will keep your feet getting wet.'

'But the flea market is only on during the day, and we are supposed to be in school,' said Kareem.

'Then we must sneak out now, while everyone is having their lunch,' replied Hamza. 'But we must be careful – if our teacher sees us, he will thrash us with his cane.'

Fortunately, the brothers were able to slip out of the school gates unnoticed by their teacher, and together they made their way to the flea market in town.

Neither Hamza nor Kareem had ever been to anywhere like the flea market before, and at first they spent a great deal of time looking around, their mouths hanging open in wonder. The stalls seemed to sell every object imaginable, from old carpets and tables to lamps and vases. But although they searched the market for a long time, the boys only found one pair of shoes, and they were for a full-grown man, and therefore far too big for Kareem.

As they wandered through the stalls, the brothers attracted quite a lot of attention. Children were not usually found in the flea market, especially during the daytime, and they were so scruffily dressed that some of the stallholders and shoppers wondered whether Hamza and Kareem might be beggars.

'You there!' cried a man standing behind a stall selling different flavoured tea leaves. 'You two boys! What are you doing here? You should be at school!'

Hamza and Kareem whirled around, their faces red with guilt; they had only intended to spend their lunchbreak looking for shoes, but they thought they must have been looking around the flea market for a few hours now.

'We were just on our way to the mosque,' said Hamza, thinking nobody could tell them off to prayer.

'Yes,' chipped in his brother, 'we are passing through this market on our way to pray.'

The owner of the next stall, which contained many books, smiled down at the boys, quite certain they were fibbing.

'It seems a funny time of day to pray,' he said, teasingly. 'It is too early for the midday prayer, *salat al-zuhr*, and yet too early for *salat al-'asr,* the prayer in the late afternoon.'

'We are going for our own prayer,' said Hamza. 'One in the middle of the afternoon.'

'But aren't you a little young to go to the mosque on your own?' continued the bookseller. 'You are not obliged to go until you are fourteen years old.'

'Well, I am seven,' said Kareem, 'so I am halfway there. And my brother is even closer – he is eight. So we are practicing, for when we are fourteen.'

'What nonsense!' huffed the man on the tea stall, turning his back on them.

But the bookseller continued to humour the two boys.

'I see, I see,' he chuckled. 'But tell me, young men, what are you going to use after your ablutions?'

'Our what?' asked the boys.

'Your ablutions,' said the bookseller. 'The ritual washing and purification of your body before prayers. Surely, if you were going to the mosque, you would take a little towel with you to dry yourself after your ablutions?'

Hamza and Kareem looked at one another, afraid their cover story was not convincing.

'We forgot the towel,' they said.

The bookseller took pity on them. 'Never mind, never mind,' he said, reaching into a book and pulling out a few sheets of old paper. 'Here, why don't you take these scraps to dry yourselves after your ablutions? I'm sure they'll work just as well.'

Hamza and Kareem thanked him and, feeling they had just about got away with their story, they decided to leave the market. They had spent so long there that almost the whole afternoon had passed, so instead of returning to school, they went back to their house, where they thought their parents would be none the wiser as to where they had been. Unfortunately, however, it was not just their mother and father waiting for them in the kitchen, but their ferocious teacher too.

'So here you are!' he cried. 'I have told your parents you have been very naughty and missed a whole afternoon's lessons, and now you both shall be thrashed.'

He bore down on the two boys, brandishing his silver cane, but their mother – who was shocked by his malice – caught his arm.

'Thank you for bringing this matter to our attention,' she said. 'But rest assured, we can discipline the boys ourselves.'

'Make sure you do,' said the teacher. 'I suggest at least ten lashes – twenty would be better.'

'Yes, yes, of course,' said Hamza and Kareem's mother, ushering him out of the door.

Although, after he had gone, she made each boy stand in the corner on one leg for twenty minutes instead. It was a dull punishment, during which they had seemingly endless time to think about what they had done, but at least it wasn't the cane.

Then later, when their mother was preparing a dinner of shish kebabs, their father emerged from his study and was informed of the boys' truancy. At first, he was very angry, but he softened when they explained they had been looking for second-hand shoes for Kareem. He even managed a small smile when they told him of the ablutions discussion they had had with the bookseller.

Encouraged, Hamza showed his father the scraps of paper. 'And look, Baba, that kindly old man even gave us this old paper in place of a towel!'

He expected his father to laugh, but instead he frowned and took the paper from Hamza's hands. Then the scholar rushed off into his study, and when his wife and two children came to see what he was up to, they found him in a state of great excitement, pulling books off the shelves and dancing around the room.

'My sons, those were not just scraps of paper given to you in the flea market,' he said, still skipping around his desk, 'they were parts of an ancient manuscript by a very famous poet. What you were given today is thousands of years old, and I think it might be worth thousands of gold coins!'

It turned out the scholar was absolutely right. The manuscript was subsequently sold at auction for ten thousand gold coins, and suddenly the family who had struggled to make ends meet were rich beyond their wildest dreams. The parents bought a bigger house, they bought Hamza and Kareem brand news clothes and shoes, and they even gave a little money to the kindly bookseller, who had cast off the manuscript without realising what it was, and although he kicked himself for his mistake, he was pleased with their good fortune. The boys were also sent to a new school, so they did not have to endure the bullying of that terrible teacher, and although they were far happier there, sometimes they were tempted to return to the flea market, and see what other treasures awaited them there.

The Merchant's Wife

Many years ago, there lived a merchant who sold the most beautiful textiles in town. As such, many women gathered around his stall, running their hands over the silk and wool on display and holding it up to the light to best appreciate its colours and patterns. When they were not trying to barter him down to an outrageously low price, these women would gossip among themselves, and the merchant could not help but overhear snippets of their conversations.

'My husband thinks our weekly shop at the market is twice as expensive as it is, because I always spend half the money he gives me on clothes.'

'I told my husband I was going to my mother's house, but actually I'm on my way to play *barziz* with my friends – it's the oldest game in the world, who can resist!'

'My husband hates aubergine, but I love it, so I chop it up really small and smuggle it into all of his meals.'

The merchant never failed to be shocked by these women's admissions, and he always felt very sorry for the poor, duped husbands of which they spoke.

'How scheming wives are!' he said to himself. 'I don't think I shall ever marry, for fear that my wife would be the same.'

Then one day, the merchant met someone who caused him to change his mind about marriage. Her name was Zolka, and she was young and beautiful, with honey-coloured hair and green eyes. She also seemed different from the rest of the women who came to his stall. She did not throw his textiles back on the display when she had finished looking at them, but folded them up neatly and handed them to him. She did not haggle aggressively for the modest material she had chosen, but recognised when they had reached a fair price and agreed to it. Best of all, she did not join in with the other women's chatter. When they spoke of the many ways in which they deceived their husbands on a daily basis, Zolka smiled politely, but then lowered her gaze, apparently unwilling and unable to contribute to the conversation.

Before long, the merchant realised he had fallen in love with Zolka, and he began to rethink his stance on marriage. He took to walking her home, offering her his arm as they went, and he even told her about the outrageous stories he overheard on the stall to amuse her. But then, when he eagerly begged for Zolka's hand in marriage, she hesitated.

'I am not sure,' she said, 'from what you have been telling me, you seem to be of the opinion that all women are schemers.'

'Most women,' corrected the merchant. 'But not you – never you, Zolka. I know you would never spend food money on clothes, or play *barziz* when you were supposed to be visiting your mother, or sneak food I didn't like into my dinner. I know you to be good and honest, and as far from a schemer as I can imagine.'

Zolka was pleased to hear this, and she liked the merchant very much, so she agreed to be his wife and they were married soon afterwards. And at first, their union was a happy one. Zolka moved into his nice house, she revealed herself to be a fine cook, and he always kept the finest cloth from his stall back for her, and looked forward to seeing her at the end of every day.

But as time went on, and women continued to gossip about their deceptions at his stall, the merchant began to entertain some doubts about his new wife. Was she really as innocent as she'd had him believe? It seemed unlikely that she alone was the only wife in all the town who did not scheme. Now he came to think about it, what did she do all day on her own? Was she taking his money, or lying to him, or sneaking food he didn't like into his meals? He didn't think she was, but how could he be sure?

Before long, paranoia had set in, and the merchant was extremely worried that he had, after all, married a schemer. So the next morning, as he left for the market, he locked the door of the house behind him, so Zolka could not leave and get up to mischief like the other wives.

When he returned that evening, Zolka was bewildered and hurt at being locked up all day, and with a twinge of guilt the merchant saw her eyes were red from crying.

'I don't understand why you locked me in today,' she said to him.

'My dear wife, it is for your own good,' said the merchant. 'I am afraid, if you are allowed to roam free, you will turn into a schemer like the other wives. This way is better – you can stay as good and honest as you are.'

Zolka could not believe what she was hearing: she was to be kept prisoner in her own house! At first, she thought it might be some strange joke, for hadn't her husband assured her that he knew she was not a schemer? But when he locked her up the next day, and the next, and all the days after that for the rest of the week, it began to dawn on her that the merchant was being serious, and he trusted her as little as he trusted those dreadful women that came to his stall.

Once she realised this, Zolka no longer felt confused or sad. Instead, she was furious. How dare he! How could he have the nerve to keep her here, against her will, when she had done nothing wrong! If he was this ridiculous about women, he shouldn't have married at all!

Fuelled by her rage, Zolka yanked up one of the floorboards under the bed, took a trowel from the cupboard, and began to dig. After a few days, she had dug a sizeable hole under the house, and after a few weeks it was a full-blown tunnel. Then she continued to expand this tunnel, digging and digging with her small trowel, until she had reached the neighbouring farm. The farmer, who was a kind, elderly old gentleman, was so amused to see this lovely young woman popping out of the ground in one of his fields that he offered her a cup of fresh milk and, after she had explained her situation, promised to keep quiet about the tunnel.

The merchant, of course, knew nothing of this, because each evening Zolka moved the bed back over the hole she had made. As far as he was concerned, his wife was confined to the house all day long, and he felt a little bad about this. He thought she must be very bored, so he decided he would set her some tasks to make the time pass more quickly.

'My dear wife, perhaps, as you are in the house all day, you could polish all of the silverware?' he suggested.

'No problem at all,' replied Zolka.

But she had no intention of doing any polishing, especially as she now spent her days walking around the nearby countryside and chatting with the gentle old farmer next door. When the merchant returned from work, however, he was very surprised to find all of the cutlery, pots, vases and even the brass bed posts as tarnished as they had been that morning.

'I thought you agreed to polish the silverware!' he said.

'So I did,' replied Zolka, 'but I was afraid, if I polished it too much, I would be able to see my reflection in them, and that would make me vain, just like those schemers in the marketplace. So I decided not to.'

The merchant could not argue with this, although he was disappointed. Then, the next day, he decided to set Zolka a different task.

'My dear wife, perhaps, as you are in the house all day, you could mend some of my shirts?' he suggested.

'No problem at all,' replied Zolka.

Only, once more, she spent the day in the sunshine, and didn't so much as look at any of the shirts, let alone take needle and thread to them. So, when the merchant returned, he was surprised to find the garments just as ripped and holey as they had been that morning.

'I thought you agreed to mend my shirts!' he said.

'So I did,' replied Zolka, 'but I was afraid, if those schemers in the marketplace saw evidence of my darning, they would think you could not afford proper shirts, and would take you for a ride. So I decided not to.'

Again, the merchant could not argue with this logic, although he was disappointed his shirts were still holey, and was beginning to suspect his wife was being a little obtuse. So when he set her a third task for the following day, he was sure to make himself clear.

'Wife, I am inviting a few fellow traders over to the house tonight,' he said. 'I want you to make us a delicious meal. I have already bought the ingredients for some delicious kibbeh. In the kitchen, you will find some minced lamb, pine nuts, saffron and other delicious spices. Make sure it is done by the time I get back.'

'No problem at all,' said Zolka.

But she was so angry with him by this point that, even though he had given her a direct command, she decided to disobey him, and spent the day picking wildflowers in the hedgerow of the farmer's field. As the merchant had promised, he came back with three venerable traders from the town, and saw – to his horror – that not only had Zolka not prepared any meal whatsoever, she had also left all of the ingredients exactly where he had put them on the table, so the meat was beginning to go bad.

'What is the meaning of this?!' exploded the merchant, furious with his wife and highly embarrassed to have nothing to serve his business associates. 'I commanded you to make us a meal!'

'So you did,' replied Zolka, 'but I was afraid that I would include an ingredient you didn't like, as those schemers in the marketplace do. So I decided not to.'

But the merchant could see now that his wife was making fun of him, and when the other men had made their excuses and left, he rounded on her.

'You are a terrible wife!' he shouted. 'You might not be a schemer, like those women in the marketplace, but you have humiliated me too many times. If you are not careful, I will divorce you!'

He meant it as a threat, because divorce was virtually unheard of in this little town. But Zolka merely shrugged and said, as she always did, 'No problem at all.' After she had packed up her bags, the hapless merchant had no choice but to unlock the front door and let her out of the house.

Once outside, Zolka considered what to do. She did not want to go back to her mother and father's house, because she didn't want to bring the scandal of a divorce to their door. So she went instead to the kindly old farmer next door, and told him what had happened. He, who had begun to think of this lively young woman as a daughter, was shocked by the bad treatment to which she had been subjected by the merchant, and together they concocted a plan to teach him a lesson.

The merchant, meanwhile, passed the next few days in a state of shock. He could not believe his wife had simply walked out of the door like that, and had not only been disobedient, she had also not been cowed by his threat of divorce. But as time went on, his astonishment turned to anger. If only he had not married! He had known, had he not, that women were all schemers? And yet, he was lonely without Zolka, and when he thought back on the first few happy weeks of their marriage, before he had locked her in the house, he was filled with sadness and regret.

Then one day, the old farmer who lived next door came to visit him.

'I hear you are getting a divorce,' he said.

'I am,' the merchant groaned. 'You see, I have come to the conclusion that all women are schemers.'

'Oh, I don't know about that,' said the farmer, reasonably. 'My daughter, for example, is definitely not a schemer.'

'I didn't know you had a daughter,' said the merchant.

'Oh yes,' said the farmer. 'She is a very good girl, and a great beauty. If you like, you can marry her instead.'

The merchant hesitated: on the one hand, he thought he should swear off women, but on the other it would be nice to have someone in the house again.

'I would have to see her,' he said. 'I would have to check she wasn't a schemer.'

'Very well,' said the farmer, nodding. 'But she is very shy, so I think the best thing to do would be to come to her room and see her then, when she is asleep.'

This was not exactly what the merchant had in mind, but he was intrigued now, and so agreed to the old man's proposition. So that night, he headed next door to the farm, up the stairs, and into a room, where he found a woman sleeping in the bed.

'Isn't she a beauty?' said the farmer.

It was dark inside the room, but the merchant could see that this girl was indeed very striking. She had long black hair that fanned out around the pillow, and her features were fine, although curiously reminiscent of his dear Zolka.

'Why, yes, she is a great beauty,' said the merchant.

'And you can tell, I think, she is not a schemer, just by looking at her?' said the farmer.

The merchant considered this. In sleep, the farmer's daughter looked very angelic indeed, and it was impossible to imagine her being disobedient or calculating. But he could not shake off the feeling that, aside from her hair, she looked like Zolka.

'Why, yes, I can tell she is not a schemer,' said the merchant.

'So you will marry her?' said the farmer eagerly.

'No,' said the merchant, tearing his gaze from the girl and looking sadly at his toes. 'I am afraid I cannot marry your daughter. You see, I am still in love with my wife.'

'Even though she is a schemer?' asked the farmer, in disbelief.

'Even though she is a schemer,' agreed the merchant.

At that moment, the farmer's daughter sat up in bed, suddenly wide awake. She pulled at her dark hair, which came off in her hand, and revealed herself to have lustrous honey-coloured locks underneath. Open-mouthed, the merchant stared at the wig, and then at the woman, who was of course his wife, and his heart swelled with love and remorse.

'I may be a schemer,' said Zolka, 'but only because you made me so! Before I met you, I was good and honest, but then you locked me away and gave me no choice but to deceive you.'

'I see that now,' said the merchant, falling to his knees. 'I am so sorry! You are not like those other women!'

But this was not enough for Zolka. 'You know nothing of those women at your stall, you know nothing about their lives!' she cried. 'You only hear one side of the story, and so you have been imagining their husbands as poor victims, when perhaps they are cruel, and don't let their wives play *barziz* with their friends or buy new clothes. Perhaps they even lock up the women they claim to love!'

The merchant had never considered this before, and it made him feel deeply ashamed to reflect on how he had judged those women – how he had judged all women.

'How can he make it up to you?' asked the farmer, who was keen to be the peacemaker to this marriage.

Zolka folded her arms and thought about this for a moment. 'First, he can polish the silverware,' she said.

'Of course!' cried the merchant. 'At once!'

'Then he can mend my dresses,' Zolka continued, 'and lastly, he can prepare a meal of kibbeh for my friends and family.'

'That sounds reasonable,' said the farmer, nodding approvingly.

So the merchant set to work, doing more than Zolka had instructed. He cleaned the whole house, not just the silverware; he bought her an entire wardrobe of new clothes, rather than mending her old ones; and he prepared a great feast of far more than kibbeh for all her friends and family – all to show how sorry he was. Zolka was touched by the effort he had gone to, and she agreed to move back into the house. And though it took a little time for her to trust him once more, eventually they were as happy as they had been at the start of their marriage, and the merchant never again thought of his wife as a scheming woman.

The Bon-Bon Girl

Once upon a time, in a kingdom far away, there lived a young woman that everyone simply referred to as 'the Bon-Bon Girl'. She had been given this nickname because she owned a little shop that sold the most delicious cakes and sweets imaginable. Among these treats were traditional desserts, such as buttery *halva*, sticky almonds, silky Turkish delight, as well as sugared nuts and fruit, but the Bon-Bon Girl had also looked further afield for her confectionery, so she also stocked more exotic fare such as chocolate and fudge and ice cream.

Yet, as her name suggested, the Bon-Bon Girl's speciality was candy, and not only would she sell paper bags full of little humbugs and lemon drops, she would also construct great edible sculptures out of sugar. One week, there might be a magnificent model of two swans sitting in the window of the bon-bon shop, and the next there would be a miniature band of musicians displayed behind the glass, their small bodies and instruments perfectly crafted from sugar that had been painstakingly blown, cast, pressed and spun by the Bon-Bon Girl.

Because making these extraordinary sculptures was always a time-consuming process, the Bon-Bon Girl only made one or two a month, and usually only for the purpose of decorating her shop – and for her own amusement. Nevertheless, the appearance of a new model always caused great excitement amongst the townspeople. Most of them could not afford the beautiful, sugary ornaments, but they always liked to pass by the sweet shop and admire the Bon-Bon Girl's handiwork, most of all the children. It wasn't unusual to find a little cluster of boys and girls outside the bon-bon shop at any given time, their noses pressed to the window as they imagined what it would be like to touch their tongues to the sweet and colourful surface of whatever sugary model was on the other side of the glass.

One day, to challenge herself, the Bon-Bon Girl decided she would create a miniature replica of the royal palace, which stood on the hillside above the town. It took her many weeks, and turned out to be her most difficult sculpture to date, for she was determined to get every detail right: the arched windows, the tall turrets, the onion-shaped domes. She worked day and night, in between making and selling her other confectionery, and at last she had completed the ambitious project, and everyone who looked upon it agreed it was her most impressive sculpture yet.

It just so happened that, a few days after the Bon-Bon Girl had put her model palace in the window, the prince of that land was riding through the town. He and his men were returning from a neighbouring kingdom, and their journey had been long and tiring. Although they were almost home, the prince did not think he could make it up the hill to the palace before he had had something to eat, and that was when he inhaled the delicious aromas of sugar, honey and butter wafting his way from the bon-bon shop.

'What is that heavenly smell?' he cried, tugging on the reins of his horse to investigate, and leaving his men no choice but to follow.

The prince had expected to see a simple, everyday bakery, the kind found all over the land, and was therefore very surprised to lay eyes upon the bright little bon-bon shop, and all the confectionery it contained. Moreover, when he spotted the miniature version of his palace in the window, he almost fell off his horse in astonishment.

'Why, that's extraordinary!' he declared. 'It's perfect! I have never seen anything like it in all my life! Who made this sugar palace?'

The Bon-Bon Girl crept out from behind the counter of her shop and curtseyed low.

'I did, Your Highness,' she said.

The prince stared at her in amazement: in comparison to her dazzling wares, the Bon-Bon Girl was small and rather plain. She was also young, and the prince could not believe that her small hands had made this work of exquisite craftsmanship.

'May I buy it from you?' he asked of her.

'Oh no, Highness, you must take it as a gift,' said the Bon-Bon Girl, who was in turn dazzled by this noble and handsome royal standing in the middle of her little shop.

'I insist upon paying for it!' cried the prince, beckoning one of his men for his purse. 'In fact, I would like to commission you to make another model, if you would be so obliged? Outside is my favourite horse, so perhaps you could craft its likeness in sugar, and then bring it to the palace when you are done?'

'Of course, Highness,' stammered the Bon-Bon Girl.

After pressing a golden box of baklava with ribbons, and some fudge, into the prince's hands, she made some quick sketches of his horse, and then set to work as soon as he had departed, feeling more pressured to create a wonderful sculpture than she had ever felt before. But she needn't have worried: one of the Bon-Bon Girl's specialities was crafting animals, and a horse was far easier than a palace.

When she brought the sugar statuette to the prince at the end of the week he was as delighted with it as he had been with the model palace.

'Extraordinary!' he said again, examining the little horse from every angle. 'It looks just like the real thing!'

In fact, he was so happy that, after he had forced some gold coins into the Bon-Bon Girl's hands, he asked her to craft him a miniature replica of the throne, upon which he would one day sit as sultan. Once more, the Bon-Bon Girl made some sketches of the object in question, which was ornate and intricately carved, and by the time another week had passed she was presenting the prince with its sugar counterpart.

'I don't believe it,' he said, holding the model throne up to the light to examine the features she had included. 'You have captured every little detail – I think you must have a little magic about you, Bon-Bon Girl.'

But in response to this, she simply blushed and shook her head.

'Now, I would like you to make me a ring,' said the prince, tearing his eyes from the throne at last.

The Bon-Bon Girl was surprised by this, for a ring was far simpler than a palace or a horse or a throne. But she did as she was asked, and when she returned to the palace the next day – for the commission took very little time to complete – she presented the prince with a perfect, edible ring, the sugar stone of which glittered like a real diamond. The prince, who seemed more elated by this than ever, took the little sculpture, slipped it onto her finger, and asked her to be his wife.

The Bon-Bon Girl was completely dumbfounded, and could hardly believe it as the prince went onto to describe how he had fallen in love with her: first for her artistry, and then for her modesty and sweetness. But he did seem to be in earnest, and she had fallen in love with him too, first for his good looks and position, and then for his boundless, almost childlike enthusiasm for what she did. So, with tears of joy in her eyes, the Bon-Bon Girl accepted the prince's proposal of marriage.

But when the prince then told his father he wanted to wed a girl who ran the town sweetshop, the sultan was not best pleased.

'A sweetshop?!' he roared. 'You, a prince, want to marry a commoner who runs a sweetshop?'

'But I love her, father!' protested the prince. 'She makes the most wonderful sculptures out of sugar!'

'What's that? Sugar sculptures?' bellowed the sultan. 'I have never heard such nonsense in all my years!'

'If you could only meet her!' pleaded the prince. 'If you could see her creations – if you could taste a little of what she makes!'

But the sultan had had enough: 'I do not want to hear another word about it. You will marry a princess, as befits your status, and forget about this common Bon-Bon Girl at once.'

Yet the ruler's stubbornness had been inherited by his son, and the prince decided that he *would* marry the Bon-Bon Girl, with or without his father's permission. So, that evening, he went to fetch her from her shop, and at dead of night they met with an imam, who married them in secret.

Unfortunately, and unbeknownst to the prince, the sultan's slippery vizier had followed him from the palace and witnessed the whole thing. Then, when the prince and the Bon-Bon Girl returned to their wedding night, the vizier headed straight to the sultan, and told him what had happened.

The sultan was, of course, very angry, and flew into a temper at his son's choice of bride. But after he had raged and stormed about it for several minutes, he slumped down on the end of the bed and said, 'Well, I suppose it is done. Now she is his wife, there is nothing we can do to change it, is there?'

But the vizier gave him a twisted smile. 'Not necessarily,' he said.

Then he related his evil plan: nobody but the imam knew about the marriage, so if the Bon-Bon Girl were to die tonight, there would be no scandal, and the prince would be free to choose a more appropriate bride. At first, the sultan was shocked by what his vizier was suggesting, but then he thought of his son's disobedience, and of the audacity of this social-climbing commoner, and he grabbed a ceremonial sword from the wall.

'I'll do it now,' he said.

Flanked by his vizier, the sultan hurried towards his son's room and gently pushed open the door. All was quiet inside, and the prince and his new wife were both fast asleep in the bed. The sultan crept towards the inert female figure, whose skin was very smooth and pale in the moonlight. He then said a quick prayer, begging for forgiveness for what he was about to do, and drew his sword.

'At least it will be quick,' he murmured, as he raised the blade high, and then brought it sweeping down on his sleeping daughter-in-law's neck.

He had expected there to be the squelch of flesh, the rush of blood, but instead the air seemed to crack with a great splintering sound, and the Bon-Bon Girl shattered into a hundred thousand pieces, which flew through the air like a storm of hailstones.

Awaking with a cry of fright, the prince sat up in bed, and saw that his new wife had broken into tiny shards of sugar.

'What have you done?' he asked his father, horrified.

The sultan, feeling slightly nauseous about what he had just done, picked a sweet fragment from his beard and examined it.

'Was she made of sugar all along?' he asked, disbelievingly.

'No,' said the Bon-Bon Girl, emerging from behind the curtain, 'I am quite real.'

Relieved, the prince hurried to embrace her, whilst the sultan and vizier simply stared at her, as though seeing a ghost.

'My husband asked me to make sugar sculptures of us, in celebration of our marriage,' the Bon-Bon Girl explained, 'one of which you just destroyed.'

'But how did you know what I would do?' gasped the sultan.

'We knew we had been followed to our wedding,' continued the Bon-Bon Girl, 'and although my husband assured me I would be safe, I slipped the sculpture of myself into the bed as he slept, just in case.'

'But it looked so real,' whispered the sultan, remembering the way her skin had shone in the moonlight. 'You have such a gift.'

Without even thinking about it, he touched the shard of sugar he was holding to his tongue, and it was so sweet and delicious that he dropped his sword, fell to his knees, and began to sob.

'Forgive me, my son!' he cried. 'Forgive me, my new daughter! I was consumed by madness – how will I ever make up for what I tried to do this night?'

He reached out his hands beseechingly. The prince, who was still very angry with his father for attempting to murder his new bride, folded his arms.

'Ask God to forgive you for what you've done,' he said coldly. 'All I want from you is a blessing for this marriage.'

'Of course I bless it, of course!' wept the sultan. 'We will throw the biggest wedding feast in the land. I will give jewels to all your guests, I will ask the greatest cooks in the kingdom to make food from all over the East – though none of their desserts will rival your wife's,' he added hastily. 'But you must forgive me, my son, or I will not be able to live with myself!'

The prince was still unsure but the Bon-Bon Girl took his hand and guided it towards his father's. Reluctantly, the prince gripped at the sultan's fingers, and promised he would think about forgiving him, on the condition that the vizier was immediately sacked and banished from the palace.

After that, as he had promised, the sultan threw the prince and the Bon-Bon Girl the most magnificent wedding feast the kingdom had ever known. Many ambassadors and other important guests travelled for days to attend, and the Bon-Bon Girl created superb sweet sculptures in their honour. Ordinarily, people would have said it was not befitting for a new princess to be so occupied, but then they only had to look at the models to know that nobody else could had made them, because nobody else had the Bon-Bon Girl's skills with sugar.

Mystery Quarters

In a desert land there once lived a rich and powerful sultan. As befitted his status, this sultan lived in a vast, magnificent palace, where the huge rooms were filled with silk carpets, crystal chandeliers, and fixtures of gold, silver and gemstones, while the gardens were full of exotic plants, and elegant sculptures and fountains. In fact, the palace was so beautiful that it was famous throughout the neighbouring kingdoms, and much admired by everyone who looked upon it.

The sultan lived in this palace with his son, Prince Nahwan. Nahwan was his only child, as the sultan's wife had died several years ago, and the ruler had been too heartbroken to even consider marrying again. This meant Nahwan was the sole heir to the entire kingdom, and as such there was a lot of pressure on his young shoulders. The prince had spent many hours of his childhood cooped up in the palace with various tutors, who not only taught him subjects like mathematics and languages, but also royal protocol and diplomacy to prepare him for his future role. Furthermore, when he wasn't bent over books, the prince's time was taken up with lessons in archery, sword-fighting, horse riding and hunting, even though those around him could see he was of a thoughtful, philosophical character, and unlikely to be a particularly forceful or bloodthirsty ruler.

When Nahwan reached the age of eighteen, his father introduced a new challenge for his son.

'Now you are a man, it is time you were married,' the sultan said. 'But we must think carefully about who is to be your bride: after all, she will rule by your side, and we must make the most advantageous match for the kingdom. She will be a neighbouring princess, for certain, but which one? I shall give it some thought.'

But Prince Nahwan barely listened to a word his father said. What did he care for advantageous matches or neighbouring princesses when, for many years, his heart had belonged to a humble girl far closer to home?

Her name was Elba, and she was a servant in the palace of the sultan. She lived in a tiny room tucked away at the back of the palace; a room so small there was barely enough room for her bed. Every day, Elba would wake in this little room before dawn, eat a simple breakfast with the rest of the servants, and then spend every hour from dawn until dusk cleaning and polishing all the gold and silver and jewels of the palace. And because the palace was so large, and the precious metals and stones so plentiful, this was a never-ending task for Elba and her fellow servants, for by the time they had journeyed from the east wing of the palace to the west, cleaning everything in their path, many days would have passed, dust would have blown in from the desert, and it would be time to start all over again.

Elba was a very beautiful girl, with long honey-coloured hair and green eyes, and it was her striking appearance that first caught the attention of Prince Nahwan. As his tutors droned on about wars in the distant past or a particularly difficult part of foreign grammar, Nahwan would watch this servant girl out of the corner of his eye, and think how very lovely she looked, despite her plain clothes and the fact she was always scrubbing away at some vase or candelabra.

When he finally found himself alone with her, he introduced himself (though, of course, Elba knew who he was) and she was so flustered at being spoken to by a prince that she blushed and stuttered and could hardly reply to his questions. Over time, however, a friendship developed between them, and when Nahwan discovered she was just as kind and sweet as she was beautiful, he found he was falling in love with the young servant girl who cleaned the sultan's palace from dawn until dusk.

So after the conversation with his father about his impending marriage, Nahwan went straight to Elba and clasped her hands in his.

'You must marry me, my dearest one,' he said. 'My father wants me to wed a princess from a neighbouring kingdom, but I will not love her as I love you.'

But Elba gently pulled her hands from his and said, as she did every time he declared his feelings for her, 'You are a prince and I am a servant girl, you know this cannot be.'

But her eyes were filled with sadness as she spoke, and Nahwan knew, even if she would not admit it, she loved him too.

Just as the sultan had promised, he soon decided upon a suitable bride for his son: the princess of the very next kingdom to the south, a dark-haired beauty named Raida. Nahwan was horrified by this choice: Raida had been one of the few children with whom he had been permitted to socialise over the years, and he knew her to be spoilt, bad-tempered and mean.

'Father, I cannot marry Princess Raida, I am in love with another,' protested Nahwan.

'Love has nothing to do with it,' snapped his father. 'You will marry Princess Raida for the good of the kingdom, not for the good of your heart. That is my final word on the matter.'

Prince Nahwan wanted to argue, but he knew there was nothing he could do: he could not cast off his title, for he had no brothers or sisters to take his place, and although the old man was stern, he did love his father. Besides, he knew Elba would never agree to marry him, not when it would cause a family rift, and potentially tear apart the kingdom. So, with a heavy heart, Nahwan agreed to wed Princess Raida, and the pair of them were married amidst a lavish celebration that lasted a whole week.

As Nahwan had predicted, his marriage was not a happy one. Despite the opulence of the palace, Raida was not satisfied with her new living quarters, and demanded more gold, more colourful carpets and bigger chandeliers be bought for her. She seemed to find her new husband lacking, for she constantly criticised and complained about him, especially when he ignored her in favour of his books. Furthermore, if even the slightest thing displeased her, the princess would fly into a temper, and shout at Nahwan or the servants, sometimes even resorting to throwing a comb or a slipper in her rage.

Prince Nahwan thought he might have been able to endure this loveless partnership, had he not known what true love felt like. But spending even a few moments with his unpleasant wife was unbearable when his heart still yearned for Elba. He had last seen her at the wedding, stood at the back with the rest of the servants, tears rolling down her cheeks. Since then, he had tried to catch a moment alone with her, but she always hurried away when she saw him approach, leaving Nahwan feeling hollow with sadness.

Despite her being his choice of bride for Nahwan, the sultan was also struggling to adapt to the presence of the new princess.

'I am sick of her shouting and screaming,' he grumbled to his son one day. 'This palace is miles long, yet wherever I go I can hear that woman screeching away about decoration.'

'Be thankful you are not married to her,' said Nahwan, miserably.

'I see you are unhappy, my boy, and I have come up with a solution to our problems: I am going to build you a palace. Then you and the princess can move in, she can decorate it however she likes, and I will not have to listen to her anymore.'

'But I will,' pointed out Nahwan.

The sultan laid a hand on his shoulder. 'Son, you have to work at your marriage, for the good of both your kingdoms. Perhaps, in your own home, you and Raida might learn to love one another.'

Nahwan thought this very unlikely, and he turned out to be correct, for if anything Raida was even worse after they had moved into the new palace. Now she had free rein, she shouted louder, threw combs and slippers further, and her decoration demands became preposterous: she wanted a carpet so long it would stretch the length of the whole palace; she wanted a bathtub encrusted with emeralds and rubies; she wanted a crystal chandelier the size of a small house. Nahwan did his best to ignore her shouting and strops, but it was difficult when they were trapped in the palace together, and leaving Elba back in his father's house had made him extremely unhappy. Now, he did not even have the chance of catching a glimpse of her to brighten his day.

One afternoon, when Nahwan and Raida had been living in their palace for almost a year, the prince walked into the entrance hall to find himself in the middle of a ridiculous scene. His wife was screaming at her group of decorators, and while this was nothing new, Nahwan saw that the huge chandelier Raida had ordered had at last arrived and, as she had requested, it was gigantic. In fact, the glittering object was so big the decorators had had to knock a hole in the wall to get it into the palace, for it would not fit through the doors. Now, they were trying to explain to the princess the chandelier was too heavy to hang from the ceiling, but she would not accept their advice.

'How dare you tell me you cannot hang my chandelier?' she shouted. 'Climb that ladder and put it up at once, or I'll have you all whipped!'

At this, the decorators stopped protesting, and Nahwan watched as they spent the best part of an hour attaching the gaudy fixture to the ceiling, which began to creak under the strain.

'There!' said Raida, when the chandelier was finally hung. 'What did I tell you? It's perfectly fine. I should dock all of your wages for insolence.'

She walked towards the chandelier and looked up at its sparkling crystals.

'My dear, perhaps you shouldn't stand directly beneath it,' said Nahwan.

'Oh, be quiet, you fool!' she snapped. 'How else am I supposed to admire the crystals. Yes, it looks very fine indeed. I will order three more. No, five more. No—'

But Nahwan and the decorators never found out exactly how many more chandeliers Raida intended to order, for at that moment the ceiling gave a great groan and the vast glittering object crashed towards to the floor, filling the princess's wide eyes the faster it fell, until she was crushed mid-sentence.

Afterwards, Prince Nahwan could not pretend to be particularly upset about the death of his wife, although his new palace did now seem especially big without the dominant presence of Princess Raida. For days and days, he paced the long corridors, instructing his servants to sell off the absurd adornments she had ordered and donate the money to the poor. Until eventually, he decided there was no use remaining there any longer, figuring that if he returned to his father's palace, he would be close to Elba again. And perhaps, given that when he had honoured his father's wishes and married a princess it had been a complete disaster, perhaps this time the sultan would allow him to choose his own bride.

'Father, now my poor wife is dead, perhaps you will permit me to marry the woman I love?' he said.

But the sultan did not let him continue. 'As I told you before, love has nothing to do with it. You will marry another princess for the good of the kingdom, not for the good of your heart. That is my final word on the matter.'

But this time, Prince Nahwan was not so accepting, and he swore to himself he would not marry another princess. Then, when he next saw Elba, and she tried to run from him, Nahwan followed her all the way to her tiny room, which he had never seen before.

'You live here?' he asked, shocked at the tiny space, which felt like a mouse hole in comparison to the vast palace.

'Do not mock me,' said Elba. 'You may be the prince of two palaces, but all I have is this little nook.'

'I would never mock you!' said Nahwan, terrified he had offended her. 'Elba, I am more in love with you than ever, and now my wife is dead we can be married.'

But she shook her head and said, once again, 'You are a prince and I am a servant girl, you know this cannot be.'

'Why not?' he demanded.

'Your father will never accept a servant girl on the throne. I can never be the princess of the palace.'

'Then I will be the prince of this little room,' decided Nahwan, looking around the tiny space. 'If you cannot live with me in my palace, I will live with you in yours.'

Elba tried to protest, but he would not be talked out of it, so in the end an imam married them in secret, and Nahwan left all the luxuries of his two palaces and moved into the tiny nook with his new wife, Elba.

As always, Elba would wake up before the sun and polish the palace's treasures from dawn until dusk, after which she would smuggle some food and a few books back to her room for her husband. At first, she fretted that Nahwan barely had room to move, that he would be bored and hungry, that he would miss his extravagant lifestyle, but even she could tell that the prince was perfectly content to remain in the little room. So while their living arrangement was not conventional, it was workable, and both Nahwan and Elba were blissfully happy to be together at last.

So the years passed, and perhaps the pair might have remained in that little room until the end of their days, had it not been for the sultan's grief. To all appearances, it seemed as though Prince Nahwan had vanished into thin air. Nobody had seen him since the fateful day he and his father had squabbled over his second marriage, and although the sultan had had the kingdom searched time and time again, Prince Nahwan could not be found. The old ruler was forced to conclude that his only son and heir had either left the land for good or – worse still – taken his own life as a result of a broken heart. Either way, the sultan was wracked with guilt at the way he had spoken to Nahwan, and as time went by he began to pace up and down the palace from dawn until dusk, lamenting the way he had treated his only child.

'Oh, my son, my son!' he would cry, as he walked all the way from the east wing to the west. 'Where is my son? If I could just know my boy is safe and well somewhere, I would sleep easier at night!'

Then one day, when she was polishing the palace treasures as usual, Elba overheard the sultan's wails and her heart was moved with pity. She put down her cloth, approached the old man, and bowed low.

'Your Majesty, I know where your son is,' she said. 'If you'll allow me, I can take you to him.'

The old man held little hope, for how could this servant girl have succeeded where all of his best men had failed? But he thought her sweet and kind, so he took her hand and let her lead him to the servants' quarters right at the back of the palace. There, she indicated he enter a tiny room, while she stood by the door, for there was not room enough for them both inside.

'My son!' cried the sultan, as he laid eyes upon Nahwan, who was sat on the bed reading and eating a chunk of stale bread. 'You are alive! But how can this be? And why are you in this little room?'

'I live here, father,' said Nahwan. 'I live here with my wife, Elba.'

The prince indicated the servant girl, who was watching the scene over the threshold, her expression nervous, for she feared the sultan's wrath. But she needn't have worried, for the old man tearfully embraced his son, and then Elba.

'My dear boy, you must love her very much, to have sacrificed all the space and luxury of two palaces for this tiny room,' said the sultan.

'I do, I live with my love. So it was no sacrifice at all,' smiled Nahwan.

'I see now how cruel I was, marrying you to that dreadful Raida, and I see how foolish I was to underestimate love – when I loved your mother so dearly I never remarried!' said the sultan. 'So come, forgive me, my son, and return to your rightful place in the palace.'

'I forgive you, father, but I will not leave this little room – my personal palace – until you acknowledge and bless my marriage to Elba.'

'But of course,' said the sultan, taking his daughter in law's hand once more, as the three of them left the little room. 'And I can already tell, when my time is over, she will make not only a very fine princess, but a very fine queen.'

The Cow and the Crow

There once lived a man so stupid he struggled to put his clothes on correctly each morning. Often, he would try to slip his socks over his hands, drape his trousers around his neck and tie his shirt around his waist, and only his wife's intervention saved him suffering a great deal of embarrassment when he went outside.

This man was a farmer, and because he was so dim he was terrible at running his farm: he would try to plant crops in rocky ground, and was surprised when nothing would grow; he would leave his sheep unattended, and couldn't understand why their lambs were snatched by wolves; and he would tramp clumsily through the chicken coop, and then scratch his head as to why all of the day's eggs were broken. As a result of this stupidity, the farm did very badly, and the farmer and his despairing wife were very poor indeed.

One day, in order to make a little money, the farmer's wife decided they should sell a cow. She chose one of their best milkers, and supervised the farmer as he prepared it for market: he brushed the cow's hide, polished the bell around its neck, and even hung a garland of flowers over its ears, although his wife had to step in when he attempted to put lipstick on the animal's mouth.

The farmer's wife decided her husband should be the one to take the cow to market, so she could keep an eye on their remaining animals without his interference. But she was concerned the farmer was too stupid for this task. What if he got a bad deal for the cow? What if he was tricked out of all of his money? What if he got lost on the way? For one as witless as he was, there were many things that could go wrong on a simple trip to market.

'This cow is worth at least twenty gold coins,' she told her husband. 'So I want you to come back to this farm with twenty gold coins in your purse. Do you understand?'

'Yes,' said the farmer.

'How many coins?' she asked, to double-check.

He thought about this. 'Five?' he suggested.

'No!' she cried.

'Ten?' he asked.

'No, twenty! You must come back to this farm with twenty gold coins and no cow,' said his poor wife.

'Twenty gold coins and no cow, I understand,' said the farmer.

So he set off, leading their prize cow by a rope. The animal looked very fine indeed, with its brushed hide, shiny bell, and garland of flowers, and the man whistled as he walked, pleased to be out in the fresh air and away from his wife and her complex demands. But the nearest town, where the market was, was many miles away, and after a few hours of walking in the heat, the farmer grew tired. When he spotted a tree by the roadside, he headed towards it, and slumped down in its shade.

'I do not think my wife would mind if I had a little rest, do you, cow?' said the farmer.

The cow, of course, did not answer, and while it grazed on the nearby grass, the man made a pillow with his hands and fell asleep.

He awoke sometime later to a noise above his head: a crow was sitting in one of the low branches of the tree, peering down at him.

'*Caw, caw,*' it said.

'Good afternoon, Mr Crow!' replied the farmer, lifting his hat to the bird. 'How are you today?'

'*Caw, caw,*' said the crow.

'I am very glad to hear it,' said the farmer, who was so foolish he thought the crow was talking to him. 'I too am enjoying the day, although I wish I did not have to walk all the way to market in this heat. It is far more pleasant to remain under this tree in the shade.'

'*Caw, caw,*' said the crow.

'Oh, but I must go,' said the farmer. 'My wife has told me I have to sell our cow.'

He gestured over to the animal. It was still eating grass nearby, which was fortunate, as the farmer had not thought to tie its rope to the tree.

'If only there was someone on this road who would buy my cow, and then I would not have to walk all the way into town,' continued the farmer, who was almost as lazy as he was stupid.

'*Caw, caw,*' said the crow.

'What's that?' said the farmer. 'Are you saying you will buy my cow, Mr Crow?'

'*Caw, caw.*'

The farmer thought about this for a few moments. 'That is very kind of you, I must say, but I need twenty gold coins for this animal,' he said. 'My wife was very insistent about that. I may be wrong, but I am not sure it is usual for birds like yourself to have any gold coins, is it?'

At that moment, the crow gave a great shake of his feathers, and a single, jet-black plume floated from the branch to the ground. The bird was probably trying to rid its feathers of dust, or perhaps it was trying to cool itself in the heat, but the dim-witted farmer interpreted the action as a response to his question.

'Are you saying you do have gold?' he said, looking at the spot on the ground where the feather had fallen. 'Are you saying it is buried down there?'

'*Caw, caw.*'

The farmer, taking this to be a yes, picked up a stick and began to dig. He dug and dug for a whole hour, until he had made a ditch around the tree, and eventually his stick knocked against something solid. It was an old clay pot, and inside there were hundreds and hundreds of gold coins.

'I've found your gold, Mr Crow!' cried the farmer, excitedly.

'*Caw, caw.*'

The farmer put twenty gold coins into his purse, which took him a while, for he was not good at counting, and then buried the pot back in the ground, covering it with earth. Then he tipped his hat to the bird on the branch above his head.

'It was a pleasure doing business with you, Mr Crow,' he said. 'I hope you enjoy your cow.'

'*Caw, caw.*'

When the farmer returned to his farm a little while later, his wife was waiting anxiously by the door.

'You are back early,' she said. 'Did you go to the market?'

'No, I only went halfway there,' he replied.

She looked over his shoulder. 'Then where is our cow?' she asked.

'I sold it.'

'To who?'

'To a crow.'

Before she could tell him off, the farmer produced his purse and showed her the twenty gold coins he had carefully counted out of the pot. Then he related the whole story of the crow and the buried money while his wife's face grew red with anger.

'You fool!' she cried. 'You halfwit! You complete dunderhead! That was not the crow's money, that was buried treasure. It was probably hidden by the bandits who used to roam that road, and you only took twenty gold coins!'

'That is how much you told me to bring back,' pointed out the farmer.

His wife gave a cry of rage and frustration, and then demanded he show her the spot where he had found the money. But although they walked for many hours, the farmer could not remember which tree it was that he had fallen asleep under, and there was no sign of either the crow or the cow.

His wife berated him all the way home.

'You fool! You halfwit! You complete dunderhead!' she said. 'Don't you see how stupid you have been? You could have brought back *all* of the coins! We could have been rich! We could even have kept that prize milker!'

But the farmer merely scratched his head in puzzlement.

'I do not see what the problem is,' he told her. 'You told me to come back to our farm with twenty gold coins and no cow, and that is what has happened. As I did not even have to go all the way to market to sell it, I think that makes me very clever indeed.'

THE SISTERS AND THE STRANGER

There once lived three sisters who were as different in appearance as it is possible for sisters to be. The eldest, a girl of ten, had a neck that was very long and thin, so much so that her sisters teased her, saying that it looked like a cucumber had been shoved between her shoulders and her head. The middle sister, a girl of eight, had a very ordinary neck, but quite an extraordinary torso, which was so pale and sparkling, her sisters decided it looked like crystal, not skin. Then the youngest, a girl of just six, who had a perfectly regular neck and torso, was notable for her exceptionally skinny legs, which her older sisters declared were like a couple of matchsticks, glued to her body.

The sisters lived alone with their mother, who was quite poor and did not have enough money to pay anyone to look after them when she went out to run errands. So one day, when the mother was on her way out to buy some food, she turned to her daughters before she left.

'I am going out to the market now,' she told them, 'and because there is no one to look after you, I want you to lock the door behind me. You may not open it again until I return. There are thieves and worse about who could cause you harm. Do you understand?'

'Yes, mother,' said the oldest daughter, with the cucumber neck.

'Yes, mother,' said the middle daughter, with the crystal chest.

'Yes, mother,' said the youngest daughter, with the matchstick legs.

So off the mother went into town, and the daughters locked the door behind her.

Then, an hour after the sisters had been left alone, there came a tapping at the door: *Knock, knock, knock!* The girls, who had been playing together, looked at one another in fear. They knew they had to keep quiet, but they could not help but wonder who was calling.

Knock, knock, knock!

'Who is it?' cried the oldest daughter, with the cucumber neck.

From outside, a melodic, female voice began to sing:

Little girls, I am so tired,
And know that you are there,
If you'd just let me rest inside,
There's something I would share.

The sisters, remembering their mother's words, knew they were not allowed to do this. But they were also curious about the person outside, who was now tapping the door again.

Knock, knock, knock!

'What do you mean? What will you share?' called the second daughter, with the crystal chest.

Once more, their reply came in song:

I've just come from the bakery,
I bought too many sweets,

So open up your door to me,
I'll give you lovely treats.

Now, the girls exchanged an excited look.

'Treats!' they said to one another. But, with their mother's warning still fresh in their minds, they hesitated.

Knock, knock, knock!

'We aren't supposed to talk to strangers!' cried the youngest child, with the matchstick legs.

For a third time, the voice sounded from the other side of the door:

But I am not a stranger, dear,
I'm practically your kin,
I know your mother, do not fear,
So come on, let me in.

'Well, if she knows Mother, she must be all right!' said the youngest child.

And, her stomach rumbling in anticipation of the sweets from the bakery, she crossed to the door, unlocked it and threw it wide open.

When the three girls saw what was standing beyond it, all three of them let out a great scream of terror. For hobbling into their house came a dreadful-looking crone, more of a monster than a woman, with wild, matted hair, warty skin, sharp teeth and a long, lolling tongue. She carried a knobbly cane, with which she swiped at the girls until they cowered together in a corner, and then cackling to herself she began to rummage through all of the drawers and cupboards in the house.

'Not much here, not much here,' she said to herself, in a croak far removed from the sweet, musical voice that had enticed them to open the door.

Then, after a long search, she felt under the mother's mattress and produced a handful of jewels.

'Ah ha!' she rasped triumphantly. 'I knew there would be something tucked away for a rainy day! Yes, these pretties will do nicely!'

'Please!' the girls begged, for they knew that the jewels were heirlooms, and the only valuables their mother had. 'Please, do not take them! We are poor!'

'*You* are poor?!' growled the crone, so fiercely that the girls scuttled back into their corner. 'At least you have a home, albeit one into which you so foolishly invite strangers. No, I am afraid I do not feel sorry for you, little girls. In fact, I think I will take your fine carpet to keep me warm in the streets!'

And with that, she clawed at the beautiful carpet under their feet before dragging both it and herself back out of the house.

Another hour went by, and the girls' mother returned to find the house completely ransacked and all three of her daughters sobbing together on the floor. After checking they were not hurt, she ran to her mattress, felt for her jewels and – to her great distress – realised that they were gone. With tears in her eyes too, she went to demand of her daughters what had happened, but they were too upset to speak sense and jabbered nonsense back at her. So, with a sigh, she decided to tackle them one by one.

First, the mother turned to her oldest daughter and said:

I can't believe this sight is true,
This chaos and this fear.
So daughter, I must ask of you:
Was there a stranger here?

But the oldest girl shook her head and said:

No, I promise,
No, I swear,
There was no stranger anywhere!

The mother was very disappointed, for she knew her daughter was lying. But before she could say anything, there was a great creaking sound and the girl gave a yelp of pain: she had cricked her long, cucumber neck, so that now it bent at a strange angle.

While her oldest daughter cried even harder at this, the mother turned to her second child and said:

I can't believe this sight is true,
This chaos and this fear.
So daughter, I must ask of you:
Was there a stranger here?

But the middle daughter shook her head and said:

No, I promise,
No, I swear,
There was no stranger anywhere!

Once more, the mother was very disappointed, for she knew her daughter was lying. But before she could say anything, there was a great splintering sound and the girl gave a yelp of pain: her pale, crystal torso had fractured, so that now her skin was marred by strange cracks.

While her middle daughter cried even harder at this, the mother turned to her youngest child and said:

I can't believe this sight is true,
This chaos and this fear.
So daughter, I must ask of you:
Was there a stranger here?

But the youngest daughter shook her head and said:

No, I promise,
No, I swear,
There was no stranger anywhere!

For a third time, the mother was very disappointed, for she knew her daughter was lying. But before she could say anything, there was a great whooshing sound and the girl gave a yelp of pain: her skinny matchstick legs had caught on fire, so that flames were engulfing her lower body.

While the youngest girl ran around in panic, her mother and sisters made a grab for her, forced her to the ground, and beat out the fire with some cloth ('It would have been easier to roll her in a carpet,' the mother told them later, 'but that too seems to be missing'). Then, exhausted and emotional, the little family slumped down on the floor, and the mother gestured for her daughters to sit beside her.

'Now, I think that you have all learned a valuable lesson today,' she told the three girls. 'I hope that, no matter what they promise, no matter what they say, you will never invite people you do not know into the house again. Do you understand?'

'Yes, mother,' said the oldest daughter, with the ugly, wonky neck.

'Yes, mother,' said the middle daughter, with the ugly, cracked chest.

'Yes, mother,' said the youngest daughter, with the ugly, burnt legs.

By and by, the matter was forgiven and forgotten, and the remorseful girls worked hard to help their mother start saving once more for a rainy day. Their respective neck, chest and legs did not recover completely, and they had to bear their abnormalities for the rest of their lives. But, as their mother often reminded them, that was the price of their lies, and none of the girls ever forgot the lessons they had learned that day.

Zena of Cedera

Hundreds of years ago, there was an army that conquered the East. It was one of the biggest legions the world had ever seen, as tens of thousands of men marched under its banners, their swords flashing in the sunlight, their shields casting long shadows in the sand. Most of these warriors had been trained from childhood to fight; they had been plucked from their parents' hearths as infants, sent to live in the mountains alongside the lions and wolves, and in that remote place they had learned the art of war from some of the finest military masters in the land. As such, the soldiers of this army were strong, skilled and bold. No man in its ranks feared pain or suffering, and each knew that if he were to die in battle, it would be an honourable and glorious death.

The king who commanded this army was called Omeza, and, like his battalion, he was respected and feared throughout the East. He was a large, muscular man with a keen hawk-like gaze, yet in spite of his fearsome appearance, and the terrifying army that rode at his back, Omeza had a reputation as being fair and intelligent. He inspired great loyalty in the many who followed him, as they revered his courage, his military mind, and the strict manner in which he ruled over his men; on the rare occasion a soldier was disobedient, Omeza's punishments were swift and harsh, but he always granted the accused a trial, and nobody could accuse him of injustice.

Great men belong with great women, and it was fitting, therefore, that Omeza's wife was just as indomitable as he. Her name was Zena, and she had once been a princess from a land he had conquered, a girl so full of spirit that when her own generals had laid down their weapons in surrender, she had continued to spit, scratch and kick at men three times her size. Omeza had held the blade of his sword to her throat and intended to capture her, as he had captured her father's lands, but he was so arrested by her beauty and bravado he found his own heart caught instead. He was determined to make her his bride, and set to wooing her – which was no easy task, considering the circumstances in which they had met. The princess was proud and independent, but the longer she spent with Omeza, the more she began to recognise a kindred spirit in the fierce and passionate king, and the more she came to appreciate the adventurous life she might lead, if she accepted his proposal of marriage.

By the time the army had moved on from that land, Omeza had a new wife and, like him, Zena was respected throughout the ranks. After their wedding, she bought herself a troop of the finest Arabian horses, and it soon became apparent to all the soldiers that she rode as well as any man. Zena also refused to remain in the safety of the back of the camp, alongside the children, servants and other wives, and instead she remained in Omeza's tent, and rode at the front of the army alongside her husband, her head held high. A lesser man than Omeza might have been mocked for having such a headstrong wife, but no one in the army dared question his judgement on anything and, besides, they liked to see the beautiful Zena leading them on their conquests, her golden hair shining in the sun.

Furthermore, as the years went by, Zena became more and more involved in army life. She would never be a fighter, but she was often present when Omeza's generals and advisors met, and even helped them with their military strategies. Again, this might have been a bone of contention – a woman playing at war – but Omeza's men held their leader in such high regard that they did not object to the near-constant company of his wife. In any case, Zena's input was often valuable, for she was logical and proved again and again that she had a head for strategy.

One night, when Omeza and Zena were feasting alone in their tent, and she had asked him to pass her a plate of figs three times without getting any response, she said, 'Husband, you are not being as attentive as usual. Tell me, what is on your mind?'

Omeza sighed and set down his cup. 'My apologies, dearest Zena,' he said. 'Today I had a young man put to death, and it weighs heavily on my mind.'

'What was his crime?' asked Zena, leaning over and helping herself to the plate of figs instead.

'Desertion,' said Omeza.

Zena gave a toss of her head. 'Then you were right to act as you did. You cannot have cowards fighting for you, and if you had let him go he might have been caught and forced to spill our secrets to our enemies.'

'Yes, that was my thinking,' agreed Omeza. 'But his older brother is Decimus, who as you know is one of my most trusted generals, and he begged and begged for the boy's life. Though I know I could not have spared him, it put me in a difficult position, ordering the demise of his kin. As I ordered the execution, I heard him mutter a curse under his breath.'

'Then you should have punished him too, for insubordination,' said Zena, her gaze hard.

'I think that would have been too harsh,' said Omeza, as level-headed as ever.

Zena shrugged, helped herself to another fig, and then did not think about this conversation for several days. At the time, the army was passing through a lush green country and, one morning, Zena woke while it was still dark, saddled her favourite horse, and went galloping towards the horizon, exhilarated by the sight of the red sunlight peeping out from behind the trees. As was often the case, she stayed out for a few hours, riding and riding until both she and her horse were tired out, and when she made her way back towards the camp she discovered that the day had now begun in earnest, and breakfast was being served.

'This is a wonderful place,' Zena announced, as she hurried into the tent she shared with Omeza. 'I rode all the way to the foot of the mountains and—'

She trailed off as she pulled aside the canvas flap, and at once a terrible sight met her eyes: Omeza was still lying in their bed, where she had left him, but while before he had been sleeping peacefully, now there was a dark wound across his throat, and the sheets were drenched in blood.

Zena's screams of shock soon turned to wails of grief as it began to sink in that her husband was dead. It pained her more than she could express, not just that he was gone, but the manner of his demise: if a man like Omeza were to die, he should fall in battle – he should have an honourable and glorious death, not be snuffed out while he slept, killed by someone too cowardly to face him in combat.

'Decimus did this!' Zena cried, when she had reflected on the matter. 'Decimus killed my husband, in punishment for Omeza ordering the death of his brother.'

The entire camp was searched for the general who had muttered a curse at Omeza, and it seemed as though Zena was right: Decimus was nowhere to be found.

In the days following Omeza's death, Zena felt lost: her father's kingdom was gone, swept up by this very army, and now her husband's rule had crumbled too. What was she to do? Where was she to go?

Omeza was buried under the largest cedar tree in the land, and when the proper period of mourning had been observed, one of the generals suggested the army move on. But Zena took Omeza's sword and plunged it into the fresh earth over his grave.

'I will not leave,' she announced. 'I cannot be parted from my beloved husband.'

The generals and advisors who knew her well pitied her, for they understood her heart was broken, and they too grieved for their great leader. But they did not see the use in her staying behind.

'Zena, this is a wilderness,' they told her. 'There is nothing here.'

'Then I will build a city,' declared Zena. 'I will build the greatest city in all of the East, in honour of Omeza.'

If she had been anyone else, they might have laughed at her, but most of these men had seen how she had bent Omeza to her will, and had benefitted from her military manoeuvring, and they knew she was not to be underestimated. So instead of mocking her, they allowed Zena her vision, and when the army moved on, a hundred or so of Omeza's most loyal supporters remained with Zena, pledging to help build her city.

Zena, of course, had no idea how to build a city. She had been brought up a princess, so knew nothing of constructing walls and streets and houses. But the land she had chosen was fertile, and several good harvests brought prosperity to the region. Markets sprung up, merchants arrived, and this new wealth attracted skilled workers, who began to build upwards from the ground. In just a few years, Zena had mapped out the boundary of her city, and soon enough houses, schools and mosques were springing up within its walls.

Zena paid great attention to the development of her city, for she had not forgotten her promise to make it the greatest in all the East. If she saw unevenly-laid stones, or an ugly window, she would command that it be pulled apart and constructed all over again. Everything, she told her workers, must be both lasting and beautiful. She wanted a city that would endure for thousands of years, and one so dazzling that travellers would journey across the world to visit it; Zena knew that this balance of provenance and aesthetics was what would elevate her city above all the rest.

Over a decade after the death of Omeza, the land in which he had died had been transformed: there were streets made of the finest marble, fountains burbling in tranquil courtyards, and exquisite pillared buildings at every turn, with great green domes that could be seen from miles away. Zena named this place Cedera, after the tree under which she had buried her husband, and which still stood at the very heart of her city.

For some time, there was peace. Zena had achieved her ambition, and she was much admired by those who lived within the walls of Cedera. She should have been content, but there was a melancholy about her, for her heart still longed for Omeza. She heard his army had disbanded over the years, but did not feel particularly affected by the news, although in time many of his men arrived at her gates, keen to make a new start in Cedera. Sometimes, Zena wondered where the traitor Decimus was, the man who had murdered her husband, but knew he would not dare to show his face in her lands. So she tried to forget her past, and enjoy the fruits of her labour instead, although she could not quite ignore her loneliness. Sometimes she wondered whether it might have been better if she'd had children, but she did not remarry, for she could not fathom the idea of loving any man but Omeza.

Just as Zena had wanted, Cedera was soon reputed to be the greatest city in all of the East. But unfortunately, she had failed to foresee that such a place would inspire much envy. All over the neighbouring lands – and even beyond them – kings and their generals plotted to march upon the city and claim it for their own. But Zena had built strong walls, and had learned military strategy from Omeza and his men, so over the years she managed to fend off attack after attack from the armies who approached Cedera.

Until one year, when Emperor Auro came. Auro was a powerful ruler, with an army many times bigger than Omeza's had once been, and just as ferocious. As he advanced on Cedera, and Zena saw the tens of thousands of men who were preparing to seize her city, her chest tightened with fear. Nevertheless, she was angry: she had not spent almost two decades building this wondrous place simply to hand it over to the first arrogant ruler with a big enough army. So Zena demanded the main gate be opened, and she walked over the drawbridge to meet this new foe.

Emperor Auro was younger than she had expected, with fine dark features that were only slightly marred by battle scars. He watched with great interest the proud woman striding towards him, her expression hard. Zena was older now, but still striking, and still in possession of that imperious nature she had had as a princess, long ago.

'I have heard a lot about you, Zena of Cedera!' Auro called out. 'Men have told tales of your beauty, that it matches that of your city – and,' Auro paused to gaze past the princess at Cedera, 'and I see they did not exaggerate.'

'I am not interested in your flattery,' she said. 'Turn your men around and be gone from these lands!'

'You must see, I cannot do that,' replied Auro. 'I am the greatest ruler in the East, and as such, I should be in possession of its greatest city!'

'This city is mine!'

'Not for much longer, I fear,' said Auro, smiling at her defiance. 'But you have a choice, Zena of Cedera. Surrender to me now, and I will take the city peacefully. There will be no fighting or looting, no destruction. No man, woman or child within those walls will be harmed.'

'And if I refuse?' said Zena. 'If we fight?'

Auro laughed. 'I sense you are an intelligent woman, so you must see this is a battle you cannot win. No matter how sturdy your walls, no matter how strong your defences, I have too many men. They will attack, they will conquer, and – if I order it – they will wreak havoc on your city. There will be fire and blood and chaos. Is that what you want, Zena of Cedera? Is that what you hoped the legacy of your city would be?'

Zena closed her eyes, realising this was no choice at all, and Emperor Auro took this as a sign of her surrender, and ordered two of his generals forward to arrest her.

She was taken back to her palace in Cedera, and although she was permitted to return to her quarters, Auro had her locked in until he had decided what to do with her. Zena threw herself onto the bed and cried furious and bitter tears, although it was comforting to hear that all was quiet in the streets outside: clearly, Auro had kept his word, and taken the city peacefully.

Then, a week or so later, the emperor came to visit her. In spite of finally getting his hands on the greatest city of the East, for the past few days he had been able to think of nothing but Zena. Like Omeza before him, Auro felt that she had been the one to capture him, and not the other way round.

'Zena, I want you to marry me,' he said.

For the first time since the loss of Cedera, she laughed. 'You have taken my city,' she said. 'You have robbed me of everything I have worked for over the past two decades – and now you want to me to be your *wife*?'

'If you marry me, you can have it back. You can rule Cedera by my side, as my queen.'

'It is *my* city!' she cried. 'I will rule it alone!'

Emperor Auro was taken aback: he had thought the lure of Cedera would be enough to convince her.

'You married a conqueror before,' he reminded her.

But this was the wrong thing to say, for at the reference to Omeza, Zena's temper only worsened.

'You are *nothing* like my husband!' she snarled. 'And my father's kingdom was inferior in beauty and power to Cedera! No, *Emperor Auro*,' she said, spitting his name as though it were poison, 'there is *nothing* in this world that would convince me to marry you.'

But Emperor Auro did not believe her. He was young and handsome, he was brave and powerful, and he was a man of great wealth and limitless resources – what woman could refuse his hand? So, he set out to prove Zena wrong, and the next day he returned to her quarters with a large wooden chest, which he set at her feet.

'Open that chest, and tell me you will not marry me,' he challenged her.

Zena bent down, opened the lid, and saw that the chest was filled with hundreds of gold coins; enough to start building a new city, if she so desired.

'Is that all?' she said, running her hands through the shining metal. 'Gold? No, Emperor Auro, I will not marry you.'

The emperor was surprised, but not shocked; perhaps it had been optimistic to imagine she would change her mind so soon.

So he took back the wooden chest and, undefeated, returned with it the next day.

'Open it now, and tell me you will not marry me,' he said.

Zena did as he instructed, and saw that the chest was now filled with hundreds of rubies, which were surely worth more than the gold of the day before.

'Is that all?' she said, running her hands through the jewels. 'Rubies? No, Emperor Auro, I will not marry you.'

For a second time, the emperor was taken aback, but he was not about to give up. He took back the chest and returned with it the next day, repeating his statement.

'Is that all?' said Zena, running her hands through the clear, glittering stones. 'Diamonds? No, Auro, I will not marry you.'

And so it went on. Every day, Auro came to Zena's cell, the wooden chest full to the brim of something he hoped would convince her to be his wife. At first, he offered her only precious stones – sapphires, emeralds, jade and pearls – but she refused them all. Then he filled the chest with silks and cashmere, furs and ivory. He sent emissaries all over the East to track down the finest wines, the best food, the most beautiful pieces of art. But Zena closed the lid on all of it, refusing his proposal again and again.

As time went on, however, she came to enjoy his visits. Although she knew she would always turn down whatever he offered her, and therefore never become his wife, it amused her to wonder what this powerful emperor would bring her next.

Sometimes, after she had refused him – which Auro found less and less surprising as time went on – they would talk a little. Zena was, of course, starved of company, and Auro was hopelessly in love with her, so they would discuss their pasts, their present, their hopes for the future. And one day, almost a year into her incarceration, Zena found herself opening up to Auro about Omeza; how they had met (and Auro noted the similarities between that meeting and this one), how she had fallen for him, and how he had been so unjustly taken from her,

'So you see now why I can never marry you, Auro,' she sighed. 'I am bound to Omeza, even though he has gone. It is as though an invisible thread links me to him, and it cannot be untied.'

After that, Auro did not come to her quarters for many days. Zena supposed he had finally given up on his desire to make her his wife and, to her own surprise, found she felt a little disappointed. Then, after a week-long absence, he returned with the now-familiar wooden chest.

'I thought you had forgotten me,' said Zena, pleased to see him, in spite of herself.

'Dearest Zena,' said Auro, placing the chest at her feet as usual, 'I think I understand you a little better now than I did a year ago. And because I love you even more than I did then, I cannot come to this room every day, and be refused again and again. So this is the last time I will come here, and the last time I will ask you: please, open that chest, and tell me you will not marry me.'

Obediently, Zena bent down and opened the lid. As she did so, she wondered what she would find inside – what his final offering would be. He had never brought her opals or amber. Or perhaps it would be something edible, like a rare fruit? She might like a pet, she thought – perhaps a little kitten to keep her company. And while these thoughts went through her head, she also reflected on what he had said, and considered what it would be like to live out her days without him; her heart ached at the idea.

She frowned as she peered inside the chest and found it contained nothing but a grubby old sack. She gagged as an unpleasant aroma filled her nostrils, and winced as she saw the cloth was splattered with blood.

'What have you brought me?' she asked, half-intrigued, half-fearful.

Auro did not answer, but watched as Zena boldly thrust her arm into the sack. Her hand made contact with something hard, cold and sticky that was covered in fur – no, she thought, *hair*. Swallowing, Zena forced her fingers to close around this tangled mop, and then she dragged from the sack a severed and bloody human head.

She gasped as she held it at arm's length, winded by the sudden sight and weight of it. And then, under Auro's anxious gaze, she laughed. In spite of its grey and bloody skin, Zena recognised this face, and she knew why Auro had done this: the head belonged to Decimus, the general who had murdered Omeza.

'Now, tell me you will not marry me,' said Auro.

Zena looked up at him, this man who had finally understood she could not be wooed by jewels or flowers or silks; who she thought might now understand her better than herself, for she had not realised, in all these years, that what she wanted above all else was justice and vengeance. Zena stood up, and as the bloody head of Decimus dropped from her hand to the floor, she felt that invisible thread between herself and Omeza unravel.

'I cannot tell you that, Auro,' she said.

He took a step towards her, hardly daring to hope.

'Tell me you will not marry me,' he said again.

'I won't!' she laughed, as defiant as ever. 'You will be my husband, and you will rule Cedera by my side, as my emperor.'

This was good enough for Auro, who finally dared to take her in his arms and kiss her. They were married the next day, and there was much celebrating throughout the city, for although Auro's rule had been as peaceful as he had promised, all the people were glad to see Zena resume her rightful position as the ruling Queen of Cedera.

The Anxious Sultan

Many years ago, there lived a sultan who was always consumed with worry. He was a rich and powerful man, whose kingdom stretched for as far as the eye could see, and yet his privileged position did not stop him fretting about every little detail of his existence.

'I am afraid my clothes look all wrong, and my people will not respect me,' he would tell his advisors. Or, 'I am afraid of hosting a party at the palace, as my guests might have a terrible time.'

More often than not, the sultan would say something like, 'I am afraid this food will not agree with me, and if I eat it I will be ill for days.' Because, above all else, the sultan was a huge hypochondriac, and so was always convinced he was at death's door: 'I am afraid I have a back ache,' he would say, 'I am afraid I have a stomach ache – a finger ache. I am afraid I'm losing weight – or am I gaining weight? I can't sleep, I sleep too much, I am having bad dreams – oh, what do you think they mean?'

Needless to say, the sultan's constant worrying put a great strain on his advisors, who spent all of their time running hither and thither to try and appease his anxiety. They bought him clothes of the finest silk, so he would feel confident in front of his subjects. They employed the top chefs and the most beautiful dancers in the land, so nobody could fail to enjoy themselves at the sultan's party. They sent for herbal concoctions and rare mushrooms to settle the sultan's stomach. And they put together a huge cabinet of medicines, and summoned the finest doctors in all the land, so the sultan could be reassured that the cut on his finger or the freckle on his knee would not consign him to an early grave.

All of these measures were extremely expensive, and the sultan's advisors spent a huge amount of gold trying to give their ruler some peace of mind. Which perhaps would have been acceptable, had the sultan's mind ever been at peace, but as his worries seemed to be so frequent and so varied, over time it became apparent that his anxiety was in danger of bankrupting the whole kingdom.

'Something must be done to make the sultan happy and stop this spending,' said one of the ruler's youngest advisors, a plucky young man called Rakan.

'We have tried everything!' wailed his colleagues, who were older and more jaded by their work than he. 'We have tried sleeping draughts and healing ointments and long walks in the countryside and –'

'But those solutions were in response to specific complaints,' interrupted Rakan. 'We suggested them to cure his insomnia and his sore ankle and his fear he was inhaling too much dust in the palace. Now, I'm suggesting we tackle the root cause of all this misery: his worrying.'

In order to do this, Rakan sent for a guru, who arrived at the palace three days later. He was an old man with a long white beard, and brought nothing with him aside from his walking stick and the clothes on his back. The guru insisted on staying at the palace for a week in order to observe the sultan, and the royal advisors waited on tenterhooks for the time to elapse, so desperate were they to curb the sultan's worrying. They imagined the old man would present them with a list of ingredients for a complicated remedy, or recommend strange practices from faraway lands, such as sticking needles into the sultan's skin or bleeding him with leeches. But instead, when the week was up, and the sultan and his advisors had gathered in the throne room to hear what the guru had to say, the old man's solution sounded relatively simple.

'Your Majesty, what you need is a Happy Shirt,' announced the guru.

'Oh yes, a Happy Shirt!' cried the sultan.

'A Happy Shirt! A Happy Shirt!' cried the advisors.

And everybody began to laugh and chatter in delight, because of course a Happy Shirt was exactly what the sultan needed – it was the perfect solution!

The only person who did not share in the excitement of the guru's pronouncement was Rakan, the youngest advisor.

'Excuse me, Mr Guru,' he called over the crowd, 'but what exactly *is* a Happy Shirt?'

'It is a shirt that makes its wearer happy,' said the guru, as though this were very obvious – indeed, there was much giggling around the throne room in response to the silly question.

'Fine, but what does a Happy Shirt look like?' asked Rakan, sceptically.

The guru thought about this for a moment, and then said, 'All Happy Shirts look different, so I cannot describe just one.'

'All right then, where can we find a Happy Shirt?' persisted Rakan.

The guru shrugged. 'I cannot tell you that either, for Happy Shirts are rare and hard to find. But I guarantee, if you track one down for your sultan, he will worry no longer.'

This was good enough for the royal advisors, who set out at once to search the kingdom for a Happy Shirt. Over the next few weeks, they returned to the palace with all manner of clothes: shirts made of silk, cotton and wool; shirts that were plain and others that were patterned; shirts embellished with shining buttons, gold thread, or precious stones; shirts that weren't shirts at all, but trousers, or headdresses or slippers that had caught the attention of a particularly desperate advisor. But the sultan tried on each of these garments and immediately shook his head with sadness.

'This is not a Happy Shirt,' he said of each one, 'I feel exactly the same.'

But the advisors were undeterred, and continued to look for the object that would solve all their problems, going further and further afield in their quest. Rakan, meanwhile, who had not presented the sultan with a single shirt, went instead to the guru himself.

'There's no such thing as a Happy Shirt,' he said. 'You made it up.'

He expected the guru to angrily refute this accusation, or else throw himself down on his knobbly old knees and beg Rakan not to reveal his deception to the sultan. But instead, the guru said, 'Young man, let me tell you a story.'

'Excuse me?' said Rakan, nonplussed.

'Listen,' said the guru, raising a hand to shush him, and this is the tale he told:

Once in a faraway land, there was a lion who ruled over the whole of the savannah. He was a ferocious beast, and he terrorised every creature he came across, just because he was bigger and fiercer than everything else. So the other animals hated this lion, and wished there was a way they could be free of him. Then, one day, the monkeys – who were the cleverest animals in the savannah – had an idea. When the lion passed under their tree, they struck up a loud conversation in his hearing.

'Did you hear about the Mouse-Monster?' one monkey said to the others.

'Oh yes, I heard it claimed another life last night – a leopard this time.'

The lion overheard this and roared with laughter. 'Did I hear you mention a Mouse-Monster?' he asked. 'What nonsense is this?'

'It is not nonsense, it is quite true,' said the monkeys. 'There is a Mouse-Monster roaming the savannah, killing animals in their sleep. You should be careful, Mr Lion.'

But the lion continued to laugh. 'He will not harm me,' he said with confidence. 'I am the most fearsome animal in all of the savannah.'

'Oh, but that doesn't matter,' replied the monkeys. 'You see, the Mouse-Monster waits until you are asleep, then it crawls up your paw, over your face, and then it nibbles through your eyeball and burrows into your brain. As we said, a leopard was killed in this manner last night, so you might be next, Mr Lion.'

Although the lion gave a snort of derision, he no longer felt like laughing. Indeed, as the day wore on, he found he could not stop thinking about this Mouse-Monster.

'I am sure it is all stuff and nonsense,' said the lion to himself, as he settled down inside his cave, 'but I will stay awake tonight, just in case.'

And that is what he did, although it was very difficult to stop his eyelids from drooping shut and not succumb to sleep.

'Thank goodness you survived the night, Mr Lion!' called the monkeys the next day. 'A cheetah was killed by the Mouse-Monster just a few hours ago, so the little fiend is definitely targeting big cats like you!'

The lion, who was very tired, was alarmed to hear this, and instead of chasing and snapping at the other animals in the savannah as he usually did, he hid behind a rock and cowered with fright. Then, that night, in spite of his exhaustion, he resolved to stay awake once more, for he could not bear the thought of the Mouse-Monster crawling up his paw and nibbling through his eyeball to his brain.

And so it continued. Every day, the monkeys would tease the lion about the Mouse-Monster, and every night the lion would retreat to his cave and try and stay awake so he would not be killed in his sleep. So before long, the biggest and fiercest bully in the savannah was reduced to a thin, ragged creature who was so weakened by lack of sleep, and so unhinged by fear, he didn't even have it in him to hunt anymore.

Then one night, as the lion was struggling to keep his eyes open, he heard a tiny scrabbling noise in his cave that made his blood run cold. He sat bolt upright, knowing there were very few creatures in the savannah that made such a small sound, and then – to his horror – a mouse scurried into view.

It was, of course, a perfectly ordinary mouse. Had he been in his right mind, the lion could have squashed it with one paw, or else scooped it up and swallowed it whole for a snack. But the lion was not in his right mind, and when that little, innocent mouse scampered into his cave, he let out a shriek of fear and fell down dead.

Afterwards, all of the animals in the savannah celebrated, and congratulated the monkeys on their ingenious plan to dispose of the terrible lion. The tiny mouse who had accidentally strayed into his lion's cave was given enough grain and seed to feed his family for a whole year, and whenever any creature in the savannah misbehaved again, he or she would always be told, 'Be careful, or the Mouse-Monster will get you.'

Once the guru had finished his tale, Rakan frowned.

'But our sultan is not a ferocious lion,' he said. 'Tell me, what is the significance of this tale?'

And the guru replied, 'Your sultan may not be ferocious, but like that lion he is ruled by fear – a fear that could well destroy him.'

'There's no such thing as a Happy Shirt,' pondered Rakan, 'just as there's no such thing as a Mouse-Monster. But in this case, the shirt could be his salvation, not his undoing.'

'Perhaps,' said the guru, with a smile.

Rakan then went on a long walk to think over what the guru had told him. He walked and walked until he had left the palace far behind, and come to a valley in the mountains, where he spied a shepherd by a stream. The thing that particularly caught Rakan's attention about this otherwise remarkable man was that he was bare-chested because he was washing his shirt in the water, whistling cheerfully as he scrubbed the tatty old garment. Intrigued, Rakan continued to observe the humble man as he laid out his shirt to dry in the sun, slumped smilingly against a tree, and watched the goats in his care gambol happily in the grass nearby.

'Why, this man seems extremely happy!' Rakan said to himself.

But he knew it was no good bringing this shirt to the sultan, because the shabby old thing would do the ruler no good – after all, there was no such thing as a Happy Shirt. But what if the sultan could be brought here, to see the shepherd?

So Rakan returned to the palace, and told the sultan a white lie, saying, 'Your Majesty, I have found a Happy Shirt. It belongs to a shepherd in the mountains, but he will not be parted from it.'

The sultan leapt off his throne in excitement. 'Take me there at once!' he instructed Rakan, 'and we will see if we cannot convince this shepherd to hand it over.'

So the sultan, Rakan, the guru, and several of the royal advisors set out into the mountain, where they found the shepherd under the same tree, playing a jaunty tune on a wooden flute.

'Oh, you were quite right – that is clearly a Happy Shirt!' cried the sultan, clapping his hands in delight. 'Now, I must have it for myself.'

He and his royal staff approached the shepherd, who looked up at them in wonder and some confusion. Then the sultan announced, 'Kind Sir, I have come to enquire about purchasing your shirt.'

The shepherd was completely nonplussed by this question. He glanced down at his shirt, which was worn and somewhat stained with grass and mud, in spite of the washing.

'You – you want this old shirt, Your Majesty?' he asked.

'Oh, don't play the innocent with me, young man, I know what that shirt is,' said the sultan, waggling his finger at the shepherd. 'So tell me, how much do you want for it?'

'For my shirt?' repeated the shepherd, still completely bewildered.

'Five hundred gold pieces?' said the sultan. 'One thousand gold pieces?'

The sultan's advisors began to whisper among themselves, wondering whether the kingdom could afford such an expense. The shepherd himself began to suspect the sultan might be mad. And because he was an honest man, and did not like the idea of taking advantage of someone who seemed slightly unhinged, he stood up and gave the sultan a little bow.

'If you buy some goat's milk for your journey back, you can have the shirt for free,' he said. 'Although perhaps you can find me a replacement, as it is the only one I have.'

Upon hearing this, the sultan's eyes filled with tears. 'For free? Do you hear that, everyone? This is the power of the Happy Shirt! It renders this man generous beyond words! No, my dear friend, I cannot accept your offer, it is too generous.'

But the shepherd was already pulling the shirt over his head and offering it to the sultan. The ruler wore an expression of great awe as he stretched a quivering hand towards the tatty old cloth, as though touching a holy relic, and then he too stripped off his fine silk kaftan and pulled the so-called Happy Shirt over his head instead.

'Praise be to Allah!' he called, casting his eyes skyward, a great smile spreading over his face. 'Oh, glorious day!'

'You – you feel different?' stammered his advisors.

'Of course I feel different!' cried the sultan. 'I am wearing a Happy Shirt! I shall never take it off, and I shall never worry again!'

After he had returned to the palace wearing the grubby old shirt, the sultan decreed that the shepherd should have as much land and as many goats as he wanted – and that any request he made of the royal advisors should be immediately met. Fortunately for the kingdom's finances, the shepherd was a modest man, and aside from insisting on a new shirt, he asked for very little. Every so often, the sultan would send him lavish gifts, which the shepherd would give to his family, and over time the two men became friends. Sometimes, the sultan would even visit the shepherd in the mountains, and the royal advisors always noted that he was very cheerful when he came back, and privately thought that these visits were far better for his mood than any shirt.

As for the Happy Shirt itself, the sultan was true to his word, and insisted upon wearing it every day, as he was convinced it was the reason he was no longer plagued by worry. As a result of this, the shirt began to get even more worn and soiled as time went by, and the royal advisors started to fret about what would happen when it fell apart completely. But fortunately Rakan – who had been highly rewarded for his part in finding the shirt in the first place – had the ingenious idea of replicating the garment, so there were seven Happy Shirts in total, one for each day of the week. If the sultan noticed that the tatty old shepherd's attire he put on every day was always mysteriously clean and smart, he did not say anything – perhaps he simply thought it was the magic of the Happy Shirt at work.

Author and Translator

Reda al-Dabbagh is a collector of Arabic literature, and has a passion for translating unpublished works of classical Arabic fiction. He comes from an important leather-manufacturing family in Syria and was educated in the United Kingdom and the United States. This is his first English translation of old Arabic folk tales.